Praise for
The View from Below

"Deep and penetrating ... poignantly appealing. This debut is likely to haunt readers' thoughts for a long, long time."
—FOREWORD **magazine**

"Crittenden has an eye for what makes siblings one flesh and bone, for the pulse and rhythms that keep them together no matter what life has brought about to separate them." —BOOKLIST

"Intricately detailed West Coast settings and a supple range of characters display Crittenden's poignant comprehension of the fragmentation of memory and how early bonds of love reverberate throughout a lifetime."
—PUBLISHERS WEEKLY

The View from Below

The View from Below

Stories by Lindsey Crittenden

Mid-List Press
Minneapolis

FIRST SERIES: SHORT FICTION

Published by Mid-List Press
4324-12th Avenue South
Minneapolis, Minnesota 55407-3218

Library of Congress Cataloging-in-Publication Data
Crittenden, Lindsey, 1961 -
The view from below : stories / by Lindsey Crittenden
p.   cm. -- (First series)
ISBN 0-922811-40-7 (alk. paper)
1. United States--Social life and customs--20th century--Fiction.
I. Title.   II. Series: First series (Minneapolis, Minn.)
PS3553.R5344V53   1999   98-50586
813'.54--dc21   CIP

Some of the stories in this collection originally appeared in the following
publications: *Berkeley Fiction Review*, "The Splendor of Orchids";
Faultline, "The View from Below"; *Quarterly West*, "Away from Trees";
River City, "Bees for Honey"

Manufactured in the United States of America

For my mother, my father, and Bo—
we are three now, but always four.

Acknowledgments

I have been lucky in friends and teachers. Warmest thanks go to Will Baker, Max Byrd, Ron Carlson, Jack Hicks, Jim Houston, Patrick McGrath, Valerie Miner, Elizabeth Tallent, Katherine Vaz, and Alan Williamson for their generosity, encouragement, and care. I am grateful also to the communities of Art of the Wild, Writers at Work, the Ucross Foundation, and Virginia Center for the Creative Arts, where several of these stories began and grew. Thanks to Greg for bird tips, and to Dylan for inspiration. Finally, to my friends, long-term and new, who have sustained me immeasurably with laughter, faith, and love.

Contents

The View from Below

EVERY NIGHT THEY ALL WENT OUTSIDE, BENJY TOO, BECAUSE
their mother said he would go crazy, allergies or no allergies, if
he stayed cooped up indoors day and night. The grown-ups
seemed too excited about the moon-landing, their voices
raised in laughter as they lifted tall plastic glasses, rattling ice
cubes and citing what they'd read about Neil Armstrong's wife,
Buzz Aldrin's kids, how the astronauts had practiced eating
upside down in the simulator.

Robin stood by Uncle Mark's diving board and counted
out loud to one hundred so she wouldn't have to hear them.
She'd turn her back on the yard, shadowing in dusk, the
embers on her parents' cigarettes glowing red against the dark-
ening lawn, the lit pool like a blue-green jewel, while Benjy
found a place to hide. The sky behind the neighbors' black
palm trees was tangerine and lavender, psychedelic with smog,
and the stars weren't out yet. She saw only the crescent moon,
tilted as if leaning back. Her father had explained to her the

phases of the moon, and she knew it was always all there—
hefty, substantial—although sometimes she saw nothing at all,
or only half of it, or, last night, a white curve like a cat's shorn
claw. Sometimes she could see it during the day, a surprise up
in a blue sky. Men were on their way there, they'd be there in
a few days, her father said; Robin would see it on TV. Robin
didn't need these explanations, these reasons to believe. She
knew from looking at it that the moon was real. It was more
real to her than the grown-ups' voices, the clunk of ice cubes
against plastic, the rustle of palm trees in the wind. *Don't get
there*, she would whisper, closing her eyes. *Make a wrong turn.*

During the day, when smog hung like a net of brown grit
over the green yard, Robin stayed with Benjy in Uncle Mark's
den, while the grown-ups lounged on lawn chairs on the other
side of the sliding-glass doors. At noon, they assembled sandwiches—tuna fish, egg salad and watercress—then disappeared upstairs for naps. It had been like this since they'd
arrived at Uncle Mark's, three days before, for a week's visit.

AT HOME, AT THE CLEARED END OF THE LONG KITCHEN TABLE
or on their living room floor, Robin and Benjy's father played
with them. He swirled puzzle pieces with the palms of his slender pale hands, the gold band glinting in the light from the
hanging lamp, dealt cards swiftly for Spit and Double Solitaire,
knelt to build forts from brightly colored cardboard boxes, to
hook together train and car tracks, to shoot marbles across the
Formica-topped table extensions Robin's mother made them
use. Here, at Uncle Mark's, he didn't. He stayed with their
mother and Uncle Mark, and, if inside, sat at the game table in
the den to play grown-up games: cribbage, dominoes.

Robin and Benjy ignored the furniture to play on Uncle
Mark's carpet, an olive-green shag that covered the living room

and den floors and climbed the stairs to the last riser outside the bedroom they shared. Benjy set up his Hot Wheels tracks and Robin lay on her belly to braid the long floppy strands that reminded her of knitting yarn. She'd started in the corner of the den, underneath the game table, and planned to braid the entire room. If the smog stayed bad, she'd finish in a day or two.

"Checking up on my housekeeping?" Uncle Mark was stepping over her on his way to the kitchen. His blue bathing trunks were plastered in wet creases against his legs, swirls of dark hair flat against his skin. Drops fell onto her bare legs. He was bigger than her father, and his deep voice boomed down to her. His chin and jaw line were peppered with stubble; the day they'd arrived and he'd bent down to kiss Robin, it had scratched her cheek. Now, his feet left damp elliptic impressions in the rug, a chain of lakes.

He passed her again on his way out and she tucked like a turtle. "Still waiting for something to grow?" He chuckled and placed his foot on the small of her back, pressed a little.

She went rigid, and he walked around her, whistling, and out the door.

Hadn't he seen how she'd parted the strands and combed them in different directions with her fingers, blocking out squares that she then braided? There was richness and detail visible only if you got down on your stomach and watched it for a while. Grown-ups stepped on it, vacuumed it, took it for granted. She supposed Benjy's activity, with its loop-the-loops and straightaways and fast little cars with whirring wheels, was more self-evident.

THE SMOG BURNED HER EYES LESS WHEN SHE WENT OUTSIDE at dinner time, although it still sat on her chest, heavily, like a dentist's X-ray apron.

"What do you want, Sugar Bunny?" Uncle Mark called her different nicknames all the time, but they sounded more like jokes than endearments.

Robin wasn't used to being asked. She looked up. "Huh?"

Uncle Mark stood over the barbecue with a pair of tongs and a long-handled brush. His hand, in a gray oven mitt, looked like a paw. "White meat? Dark meat? Thigh, breast, drumstick?" He painted each piece with a smear of red sauce and stepped back out of the smoke, tapping the tongs against the rim of the barbecue bowl like drumsticks, a clangy beat.

"She'll take anything, Mark."

"Yeah, but what's she want? Robin?"

Robin looked at her mother, who was leaning over, ripping plastic from the bundle of paper plates. "I want the drumstick, please," Robin said.

"There you go!" He smiled widely and raised his tongs to point them at Robin, then lowered them to close in on the drumstick, lifting it from the grill and through the smoke to drop it onto the paper plate Robin's mother had handed her. Robin could feel the weight of the meat in the center of the flimsy paper plate.

"She knows what she wants, Janet, doesn't she?" Uncle Mark winked at Robin. "Don't let your mother tell you different. How will you grow up if you never get a chance to say what you want?"

"She'll grow up just fine." Her mother drew Robin to her hip. The paper plate tilted, and the drumstick fell on the ground.

Her mother laughed. "Well, she'll learn disappointment, too. Here you are, sweetie, take the breast." Her mother gestured toward Uncle Mark's tongs as they closed in on another piece of chicken, this one squarish and flat.

Robin shook her head. "I want a drumstick."

"What do you say?"

"I want the drumstick, please."

"Okay, pick it up and wipe it off."

"But it's dirty."

"Of course it's dirty. You dropped it."

"I said what I wanted. I'm a grown-up."

Robin's mother arched an eyebrow. "Oh, you are. My, how fast you've grown."

"Ouch, Janet, come on. Here's another drumstick, Robin Redbreast."

"Since when is being rude being mature?" Her mother's voice had sharpened, but Robin knew the question wasn't directed at her. She watched the tongs move in on the second drumstick but not yet lift it off the grill, and then her mother's laugh burst out, something new and strange in its tone, a way she didn't laugh at home. Uncle Mark must've done something with his face; Robin hadn't seen it but she could imagine one of the faces—lifted black eyebrows and flared nostrils, eyes wide—that had made her mother laugh before.

Her mother slapped at Uncle Mark's arm, and then he laughed, too, and Robin heard her mother's voice, still caught in laughter: "Remember that time at Daddy's club, when you...oh, Rob, when we were kids—"

But Robin was already running off, around the pool, and didn't hear the rest. She got the second drumstick, but not without a reminder to thank Uncle Mark, and they carried plates of chicken inside to eat with her father and Benjy, who'd been watching the Dodgers.

UNCLE MARK'S CHILDREN LIVED WITH MARJORIE, HIS WIFE who wasn't his wife anymore. She didn't even come inside when she dropped them off for dinner the next night, but just pulled her big yellow car onto the driveway and then backed out again and disappeared down the street. Robin didn't get to see if Marjorie—she'd never called her "Aunt"—looked the way she remembered, a TV mom: blond hair that didn't move, a dress that pinched her waist and then flared wide, matching high heels.

Robin was put in charge of the kids' table, the glass-topped one on the lanai, while the grown-ups sat around the polished mahogany table in the dining room. Uncle Mark had invited the neighbors from across the street and their kids, who'd played with Robin's cousins when they'd lived here. There were twelve people under Uncle Mark's roof, five of them younger than she, a fact that made Robin giddy with responsibility, and when she finished eating, she got up to walk through the French doors to the dining room, her back straight, head high, to announce that under her watch no food had spilled, no glass had broken.

But when she reached the open doors, and the step up from the flagstone to the shag carpeting, she stopped. She was dazzled by the adult laughter, the light reflecting off the cut crystal glasses filled with golden liquid, the scrape of knives against plates. None of the grown-ups noticed her, and when she looked back to the kids' table, her brother and cousins and the neighbor kids had all left their chairs to run around the room, to gather around Benjy's car track in the corner. She stood in the open doorway and wobbled her weight from one foot to the other, from carpet to flagstone, before turning to walk into the living room, where she continued braiding the rug, the voices of adults and the noises of children just beyond the walls.

ON THEIR FIFTH DAY AT UNCLE MARK'S, THE SANTA ANAS came and blew away the smog, and the brown mountains were suddenly visible in crisp profile against a blue sky. The five of them spent the whole day outside. Robin spread her towel along the edge of the lawn next to the hot cement coping, and peered into the dichondra. She pressed her cheek against the nubby loops of her towel, trying to get eye-level with the world hidden in the dense, springy leaves. She imagined herself an ant, the ground cover a jungle as thick as those in the movies she'd seen in school about New Guinea or the Amazon. She pulled through its tight leaves to find twigs and small white flowers and guzzling bumblebees against damp black dirt. Dichondra held moisture longer than ordinary grass, her father had told her, and it didn't require mowing. That's why so many yards in Southern California had it. It wouldn't do well in cold, foggy San Francisco, where they lived. No matter how hot the sun shone, Uncle Mark's lawn was always cool and soft, like lying on a blanket of shade.

"Mommy! Watch!" Benjy stood a long green expanse away, on the top step of the shallow end of the pool, his red trunks hanging to his knees, wet hair stuck to his forehead. The grown-ups sat by the deep end, dropped sections of the *Los Angeles Times* lifting from the lawn at their bare feet and blowing against the webbed lawn chairs. Her mother waved at Benjy.

Earlier, when they'd first come outside, their mother had smiled down at Benjy, touching his dark head with a tanned hand. "Now this is a vacation for you, too, huh, honey?" she'd said. "You were beginning to wonder if we'd dragged you down here just to have your eyes puff up. Smog is awful." And then, looking at Robin, who'd followed her out the sliding-glass doors, she said, "We might not have a pool at home, but at least we don't have smog." Uncle Mark had interrupted, "Hey, hey, I'll send you home if you don't stop knocking L.A." But their mother had just ruffled Benjy's hair. "We'll see about *that*," she'd said.

"I'm watching," she called now, but Robin, her chin propped on her fist, saw by the tilt of her mother's white visor that she had turned her head to say something to Uncle Mark. A splash sounded from the pool, and Benjy's wet head burrowed at the water's surface as he kicked back toward the steps, and then popped up, dripping water, as he found footing. Robin sat up to see her mother turn her head just as Benjy blinked his eyes toward her.

"Very good, honey." Her mother was clapping. Uncle Mark yelled, "Nine point oh." Robin's father had lowered the sports section to watch the whole thing.

"Mommy, watch!" Benjy called again. Their mother's laugh rang out, loud and sudden, and Robin realized for the first time how much it sounded like Uncle Mark's, the way girls at school sounded the same when they grouped in tight circles, laughing as they looked over one another's shoulders. *Shut up*, she thought, as if one of them had made a joke at Benjy's expense. The things they said to make each other laugh never seemed very funny, and besides, they were the only ones laughing. Robin knew her father was funny, too; she'd seen him at parties at home, his mouth curled up on one side of his smooth, rounded face and his brown eyes friendly behind his glasses, but she couldn't think what his laugh sounded like. It came out more in a tone of voice than in actual laughter. Her mother and Uncle Mark guffawed.

"Mommy!" Benjy's voice was now a shriek.

"Yes, I'm watching." And she watched as Benjy repeated his feat, the splash, the quickly burrowing head, the straight, flailing arms. Uncle Mark stood up and walked to the side of the house, where he bent over to turn a faucet and pick up a hose, and began to move around the lawn with his heavy tread, leading a stream of water from rose bed to potted begonias and geraniums. Robin watched her mother's visor follow him, her father's face hidden again behind the baseball stats.

The night before, Robin had awakened suddenly in the middle of the night. She had to pee, but she knew that wasn't what had awakened her. At first she didn't know where she was, but then the line of light at the base of the closed bedroom door reminded her. Footsteps climbed the stairs slowly, and a door slammed. She heard voices raised and vibrating through the walls. She got up from the bed and eased open the door, tiptoed toward the bathroom. Through the closed door of the room her parents were using, her father's voice was angry, clipped. "No room for anyone else around you two," it said. "You speak your own private language. God forbid anyone else should try to learn it."

Robin didn't recognize his mocking tone; she leaned one bare foot on top of the other and bent her head closer to the door. Her mother's voice was tremulous, skittering downward to make what she said a statement instead of a question: "What are you talking about."

"Oh, Janet, you know what I mean." The mockery was gone now, and her father's voice sounded resigned, worn out with being patient. "Laughing at those jokes, waiting for his approval, hanging on his every word. The rest of us might as well not even be in the room—"

"You are ridiculous." Her mother's voice was steely now, flat.

"It's true, it's true. If I didn't know better—"

"What? What, Bill? Say it."

"I'd be jealous."

"You are jealous. You are a ridiculous man."

Say it, Daddy, Robin had thought. *Say "It's you I love,"* remembering one day years before when she'd walked in on her father spinning her mother around the kitchen floor, catching her to him around the waist, singing in her ear, "It's you I love and only you, under the moon and under the sun," her mother correcting him between gasps of laughter, "*Beneath* the moon and under the sun," "You *are* the one," blush-cheeked and toothy in a red seersucker dress.

But Robin had heard nothing, nothing but her mother's voice, caught on a sob at last: "He's my brother, Bill, my big brother."

Robin ran on the hot pavement to the pool, where she sat at the edge of the shallow end and applauded Benjy. "Look," she said, when he came to her side. "Watch this." She dropped into the pool, pushing through water that killed all outside sound and stung her open eyes, pressed her hands into pale, wavering starfish against the smooth bottom, and kicked her legs up into the air and what felt like a perfect handstand.

IT WAS ONLY FIVE O'CLOCK AND ALREADY BENJY HAD BEEN locked out of the lanai for using highball glasses to support his Hot Wheels tracks. Two glasses had broken on the flagstone paving. The smog was back, full alert Uncle Mark had announced at breakfast, the weight again clamping Robin's chest when she stepped out of the house to bury her toes in the lawn and look at the calm and empty pool, Benjy yelling behind her that he wanted to come, too. They were inside now for the rest of the day: Benjy because it was dangerous for him to go out, and Robin because her mother had told her it wasn't fair to leave him alone with a babysitter he didn't know. The grown-ups were dining out.

Now he was somersaulting down the stairs, shrieking, and racing cars down the banister. Robin had done a headstand on the floor at the base of the stairs, her skull cupped neatly in the curve of the riser so the edge of the first step just met the base of her neck. She'd flung her legs up and over to rest against the slope of the stairs, and was enjoying the upside-down view of the room, the buzz in her head of too much rushing blood.

She heard Uncle Mark on the stairs, and could just see the quick sidestep of his polished shoes on the landing to avoid stepping on Benjy's cars, his fast grab of the banister to keep from getting tangled in Robin's legs.

"Dammit," he said, and Robin tucked and rolled out of his way. "Try to pay attention, would you?" he said to her, and although he patted her head with his meaty palm when she sat up onto her knees, she felt small and punished.

Her parents came down the stairs then, looking like strangers in a full-skirted pink dress and a white dinner jacket. Her mother bent over. Robin felt a silken, powdered cheek against hers, and wrinkled her nose at the accompanying wave of perfume.

"That's not a kiss."

"I'll smudge lipstick on you. Goodnight, you two." Her mother smiled. "Be good."

Benjy had landed downstairs, his head pushed against the riser in imitation of Robin, but his neck was too short to fit. It hurt Robin just to watch.

The babysitter's name was Kim. She walked past Robin and Benjy into the den, where she turned on the TV and sat down on the couch with her feet on the cushions. "Where's Mrs. Reinhart?"

Robin stood in the doorway. Her uncle's last name was Reinhart; it was what the "R" on the monogram on her mother's towels at home stood for. But the "F" on the towels was the biggest letter. Her mother was Mrs. Ferrin. "What?"

"Your aunt, where's your aunt? Doesn't your uncle have a wife?"

"They're divorced." It seemed like a dirty word, like *fuck* or *prostitution*, that she wasn't supposed to know, and Robin wondered suddenly if she'd get in trouble.

Kim turned back to the TV.

"Hey," Robin said. "We're not supposed to put our feet on the furniture."

Kim shrugged and swung her feet onto the floor.

Robin sat down at the opposite end of the couch, and Benjy lay at her feet, where he curled around his car, making sputtering and revving noises. When "The Dating Game" started, Kim talked about how she was going to get on the show, to meet a really cool guy who'd drive a Corvette or Mustang. She was saving her money for a fringed suede vest to wear on the show.

"You'll be dating in a few years," she told Robin. "Then you'll understand. You have to be choosy. You can't go out with just anyone. You have to know the questions to ask, the way to present yourself."

Robin had no idea what Kim was talking about. "I'm nine," she said.

Kim pointed to the screen. "You have to be eighteen to get on the show. I only have three years. I'll have my license next year, but it's better to have a boyfriend with a cool car. You can date at twelve if you're mature enough. I was."

"I don't want to."

"You will." Kim sat up suddenly to look at Robin. "You want me to paint your toenails?"

"Maybe." Robin looked down at her bare feet. "What color?"

"Well, I don't know. Red? Let's see what your mom has." She jumped up. "Show me."

"I'm not allowed in my mother's things."

"Oh, please." Kim rolled her eyes.

"I'm too young to wear make-up. I'm nine," Robin repeated.

"So? You going to stay nine forever?"

"I don't want nail polish anyway."

"Suit yourself."

Benjy had stopped playing and was staring at Kim, who bent down toward him. "What do you think?"

"He doesn't want his nails painted either." Robin tried to match Kim's tone of voice, but she felt a twist in her belly, like when Sandra Ellis had talked her into playing doctor and Mrs. Ellis found them in their underwear in Sandra's bed. She could tell from the way Benjy was watching Kim, his blue car stilled in his small clenched palm, that he was considering betrayal. She could hear her mother's voice: *You're the oldest. Set an example.* For an instant, she hated them all.

Benjy lifted his car up toward Kim. "Make it red. Like Racer X's."

"Okay, we'll see what we can find without Miss Priss."

"Benjy, come on. Stay here. I'll let you use my felt pens."

"I want my car red," he shouted as he ran out of the room behind Kim. "Red is fast."

Robin wanted to tell: to be a tattle-tale, a fink, Miss Priss. She'd go outside and hide behind the bamboo fence or in the soft dirt beneath the camellias: Kim wouldn't find her, Benjy would be inside without her, she'd stay hidden until she heard Uncle Mark's car pull into the garage. Word would spread around the neighborhood, and Kim would never get another babysitting job. She'd never get on "The Dating Game." But Robin stayed inside, staring at the slice of bright sun that came through the sliding glass doors where the orange curtains didn't quite meet.

She heard footsteps down the stairs and then the refrigerator door open and close, the crash of a broiler pan, Benjy's whimpering voice. Robin found Kim in the kitchen ripping open a bag of potato chips, Benjy at the table, his head on folded arms, an extended finger pushing his car around the Lazy Susan. The car was still blue.

"Your parents use rubbers." Kim pulled a small square packet from her jeans pocket and tossed it on the counter. "You know what that is?"

"I think you should put things back that don't belong to you."

"There's plenty more where this came from." Kim laughed. "They must fuck a lot." She reached into the bag of chips, stuffed some in her mouth.

Over Kim's shoulder, the cereal boxes stood on top of the refrigerator. Robin remembered her mother, at breakfast, reaching up for the Shredded Wheat, her father bending beneath her arm, leaning into her terry-cloth-shrouded hip, to pull the orange juice from the refrigerator shelf. "They do not," Robin said.

Kim laughed, a loud high bark. "Where do you think you came from? And the little whiner here?" She pointed at Benjy, slumped over his car, not listening.

Robin felt her face flush with warmth. "I think you should shut up. You can't call my brother that. And you can't say that about my parents. You're just a babysitter. You're here to take care of us." Robin walked to the table and sat down across from Benjy. She placed the salt and pepper shakers a few inches apart and laid a knife flat over their perforated tops.

Benjy shot his car through the arch. "She said she'd make it red."

"I didn't make any promises." Kim repocketed the packet, licked crumbs from her fingers. "I said I'd see."

Robin shot the car back. "You have to make our dinner. We want hamburgers."

"I know. Your mother told me. You'll get hamburgers."

"We always eat at six. Six-thirty at the latest. Don't eat all the chips."

Robin stood and Benjy followed her out of the kitchen, lifting his car up at Kim as he passed her. "You said you'd make it red."

ROBIN WOKE TO A PRESSURE AGAINST HER LEG, A CHANGE IN the slope of the mattress, woozy murmurings. Light from the upstairs hall came through the open door in a slice, shining as far as the cot across the room where Benjy lay sleeping. Her mother was sitting on the edge of the double bed where Robin slept, her father standing beside her with his hands on her shoulders. Something was wrong.

"Hello, sweetheart. We woke you up. Oh, Bill, we woke her up." Her mother's voice was thick and strange, as if she were talking through ice cubes, and a bright smear of lipstick smudged one of her large front teeth. Her hands patted the white chenille bedspread, trying to find Robin's body, and, reaching for the folded-down edge to pull it closer round her daughter's arms, missed and grasped only their own palms. "Whoops-a-daisy." The bleary smile came closer, and Robin turned her face into the pillow.

Her father cleared his throat, spoke softly. "Come on, Janet. Let's let Rob go back to sleep."

"My baby girl. My sweetisht little girl."

Robin turned her face back up toward her mother's, toward this smile she'd never seen. Her mother's eyes were hooded, lids low as if she were falling asleep. She kept saying how much she loved Robin, how proud she was, while Robin's father's slender hands clamped each shoulder. One cap sleeve had slipped down her mother's arm so that a bra strap showed bright white in the light from the hall. Robin had meant to tell on Kim as soon as her parents got home, but her determination fell away in face of this stranger's smile, these words she wished would stop.

"DADDY?" SHE OPENED THE DOOR SLOWLY. HER FATHER WAS in his plaid bathrobe, pulling a comb through his wet hair and staring at himself in the mirror. On the dresser sat a cup of coffee. One twin bed was made, neatly; the other stripped down to the mattress pad.

"Morning, pumpkin."

"Mom's in my bed."

"Yes, I know."

"Why?"

He put down the comb, turned to look at her. "She was sick in the middle of the night, so we moved her in with you. You were sound asleep."

"Did she barf?"

"Yes."

"In her bed?"

"Yes."

"What if she barfs in my bed?" Robin's voice cracked.

Her father took a sip of coffee. "She won't."

"How do you know? You think you know everything, but you don't." And, seeing the beginning of a smile tug at the corner of his mouth, she repeated: "You don't!" Outrage washed over her. "When I had the flu last year, I threw up five times in one night, remember?"

"Hey, it's okay." Her father reached out to touch the top of her head. "She won't get sick again, I promise. I'm sure of it."

Robin chewed the inside of her cheek, thought of her mother's slurred words, her smudgy smile. "What's wrong with her?"

Her father sat down on the stripped bed, and his bathrobe parted to show the hem of white boxer shorts, a pale, almost hairless leg. His head was bowed, and the straight line through his wet-darkened hair looked whiter than flesh was supposed to be. He pulled the coffee cup to him and held it for a while, looking into it as if considering medicine he didn't want but knew he needed, then took a sip and looked up at Robin. "It's something that happens to adults sometimes, Rob. It's out of her system now, honey. She'll be fine. She just needs to sleep." Robin peered at her father. She wrinkled her nose. "She smelled bad."

Her father took another sip of coffee, watching her with his brown eyes magnified through the thick clean lenses of his glasses. "Sometimes people do things they don't mean to. Sometimes adults make mistakes." No joke was tucked in the corner of his straight mouth, his smooth cheek.

Robin turned her head away and looked out the window to the heavy-boughed willow tree, the lanai roof that extended from the house, the only part of the downstairs that had no upstairs above it. She shook her head; she wanted her parents to be steady and true, just as they had always been: parents.

"Robin, honey, your mother had too much to drink."

There was a word for that, she knew: *drunk.* It was another one of those words, like *divorce,* like *fuck:* adult words. Trick words. It was bad enough that Kim had used them, but she'd never see Kim again. Now her father was speaking this way, turning everything upside down. She hated these words; they were as heavy and unwanted as Uncle Mark's foot on her back. She wanted only words that were clean and neat and meant no more than what they said. Through the glass panels in the lanai roof, the hard flagstone was a wavy blur, and she pushed away a tear so hard that she felt her cheekbone against her knuckles.

"You may as well hear it, you're old enough."

Robin covered her ears. "No, I'm not." She heard her voice, raised, wobbly, choked with tears she hated: "I won't hear it! Don't tell me!"

"Sweetheart, listen to me." Her father put down the coffee cup and reached for Robin, drawing her to him. Her body stiffened in the crook of his arm. "Your mother didn't mean to scare you. She had too much to drink. These things happen.

People seem different when they have too much to drink, but it's nothing to worry about." Robin felt suddenly chilled against her father's bathrobe. She had started to shake. "Shh...shh...," her father whispered, soothingly. "She's going to be fine. It won't happen again." He held her as she stared over his shoulder at the mattress pad, the uncased pillow, its safety tag curled and worn. He patted her back, and when he pulled her away from him to look in her face, his voice was back to its usual friendly tone. "I want you to do something for me. I want you to try to keep quiet this morning, would you do that? And keep your brother downstairs? The air's much better today, so you two can try it outside." He lifted his thumbs to smooth her eyebrows. "Everything's going to be fine. Now run along. Uncle Mark's making waffles with Benjy. I'll be right down once I get dressed."

Robin crept back in her room on the way downstairs. Her mother slept curled on her side, her mouth wide open like a child's, her brown hair tangled across her brow. Robin walked quietly around the bed; the sheets were pulled up neatly to cover her mother's shoulders. Against her tanned skin, they were clean and white.

"ROB, COME QUICKLY!" HER FATHER HAD OPENED THE SLIDING glass doors just enough to beckon to her. "It's on!"

They'd been in there for what seemed like an hour, her parents and Uncle Mark and Benjy too, who had been told not to overdo it his first day back outside, ever since lunch, watching TV, waiting for the astronauts to land. Robin stayed outside on a towel, slapping at flies and burrowing her fingers and toes into the dichondra. Above her, the sky was empty and blue.

"Rob, you're missing it. Come on."

She stood slowly, stretching, and trailed her toes against the dichondra leaves as she walked. The dimness of the den after bright sunshine stopped her just inside the door, the chill of the room pulling tight her sun-warmed skin.

"Close the door, Rob!"

She pulled the handle until it clicked shut, the curtains swishing back in place against her hand. Her mother and Uncle Mark sat on the couch, holding tall glasses of tomato juice. Her father stood near her mother, hand jangling the change in the pocket of his shorts. Benjy ran around the room, blasting his car off the game table, the arm of the couch, the top of the TV.

"Benjy, out of the way," her father said. "If you want to watch, sit still."

Her mother patted her lap and Benjy climbed onto it. He leaned back against her chest and she held him by the knees and looked at Robin. "This is history in the making, you two. You'll tell your grandchildren about this."

Robin couldn't see the moon in the small square of the screen, just a cloudy white shape surrounded by darkness, like teeth in a dentist's X-ray.

"That's the module," her uncle said, pointing to the screen. "The Eagle."

He was standing now, too, and both men watched the TV the way Robin had seen her father do in the final seconds of a close football game. Dangly spider legs hung down from the white shape into the blackness.

"I don't see the moon," Robin said suspiciously, but felt a lilt of hope.

Her father said nothing, but reached out to run his finger along the bottom of the screen, above the lip of molded black plastic, where she could just make out a fuzzy paleness.

Static interrupted the deep-voiced broadcaster, and the spider legs touched the fuzziness that was supposed it. Robin turned away. The orange curtains were drawn against the afternoon sun, and she looked through their pattern of squares, thin like worn toweling, to the palms moving above the neighbor's fence. Although the door was closed she could hear the papery rustle of their heavy leaves.

Away from Trees

It's past seven o'clock, but dust still hangs over the parking lot from the last of the tourists to leave. I have been driving since three, and am exhausted by the climb from the basin floor, by the relentless sunshine beating on the hood of the car. Already my skin itches and pulls with dryness. Just this morning, I left Connecticut: lush and dense, claustrophobically green, all lawn and hedges, soaring elms and maples against a sky matted into white glare by humidity, air that doesn't move, air that clings to your skin like a damp, thin sponge. I will have to take it easy here. I will have to go to bed early, get plenty of rest, give my body time to adjust. I will have to wear sunblock constantly, and a hat.

A ranger walks up as I'm opening the trunk, raising his right hand before he is close enough to shake mine. His hat hides his eyes. "You must be the archeologist from back east."

"Yes," I say, and smile into his face, visible now as tanned and wrinkled, with cloudy green eyes and one gold front tooth. "Holly Kincaid." I shake his hand.

"Earl Cobody. You'll be staying with Dawn and me." He must have been watching me look around, at the bare brown hills, scraped above the old blue-gray mine into white rock exposed like scars, at the dusty sagebrush tangled along the edge of the parking lot, at the wooden buildings of town straight ahead, because now he says, "There, behind you, the old burial ground. And over to the right, the Chinese camp, where the laborers lived. Then that's it. That's Bodie. Quite a town in the 1870s and '80s. By 1915 most mines shut down, and everyone gone for good after the last big fire, forty-six. Except for us, of course. And we're seasonal, most of us, only here April through October. High today of eighty-three, though of course it feels much hotter at this altitude. Low was twenty-seven, just before sun-up."

"Twenty-seven?" The warmest thing I packed is a sweat-shirt.

"Don't worry. The house is heated. Bodie may be a ghost town, but inside the rangers' houses, all the comforts of modern life. Dawn wouldn't have it any other way." He picks up my duffel, waving off my protest. I slam the car trunk and follow him, carrying my workcase.

"Lots of people say Bodie's haunted. At one point known as the most dangerous town in the West. Lots of killings. No law to speak of. Ghosts still here, seeking revenge. If you believe that sort of thing. Here"—he moves down a narrow dirt path—"this way."

We pass house after house now, all weathered brown clapboard, windows broken or boarded over, crumbling chimneys, split and sagging front steps. Outhouses beyond, and, on a small island of dried grasses, an old well. Nothing grows taller than my knees. In front of each dilapidated structure, there is a small post carved with a number that corresponds, Earl tells me, to a description in the printed tourism pamphlet. We turn another corner past a large brick building. "The courthouse," Earl says. "Only brick structure in Bodie."

"How'd they bring the bricks here?"

"Same way they brought the wood. Pain in the ass."

"Frontier justice needed every edge it could get, I guess."

He laughs, a short burst that surprises me with its friendliness, and then abruptly asks, "How long you here?"

"Probably a week or two, depending on what I find. If there's more obsidian, it might take a month."

Earl stops in the middle of the road and turns around, drops my duffel in the dirt, points his finger to the hills and, beyond, the snowy tops of mountains.

"Nevada?" I say.

He peers at me. "You don't say it like an easterner. *Nevah-dah.*"

"I grew up in California. I've just lived in Connecticut since college."

He nods. "You're right. That's Nevada. We're seven miles from the border. But before that, see that rock?" His finger ticks back and forth along the scars. "That's Bodie bluff, where they found the obsidian. Federal land. That's where you'll dig."

"I won't dig very far. About an inch."

"There'll be some grumbling if you find anything. Some people want to mine again." He shrugs, but I can see he's watching me keenly. "Nothing personal."

"Of course."

He peers at the hills again. "Gold's what built this place. And half of it's still up there. Nothing now but tourism." He picks up my bag, walks on. I turn around to follow, and notice two men who weren't there before, sitting on the courthouse steps, looking our way. One wears a baseball cap and has a droopy mustache. The other's face is hidden by the shadow of his friend's torso, and his legs, long and muscular, stretch out over the wooden steps.

"Glad to see you boys hard at work," Earl calls out, and they laugh.

"Day's over," the one with the mustache says. "But not if you're training for bellhop. Didn't know we had a visitor." He smiles and lifts his cap, shows teeth as small as corn nibblets.

"If you didn't drink so much, you'd remember what I tell you. This is Holly, the archeologist that Parks sent. Holly, this joker's Dan, and this is Craig." We are standing at the edge of the boardwalk now, and I flush with surprise as Craig leans forward and I look into blue eyes, a long straight nose, lips that look puffed, soft. His eyes meet mine just longer than would be expected in an introduction, and when I shake his hand I notice how broad and smooth his fingernails are, how the blood runs under the skin of his arm in raised ropes of vein.

I WAS WORKING ON A SITE ON THE HOUSATONIC LAST November. Three of us were camped out in two trailers five miles down river from the covered bridge where idling cars lined up for photo opportunities, just around the bend from the spot where a bulldozer turned over shards of Indian pottery while digging a tennis court.

I had taken skeins of blue mohair and my needles with me to Cornwall, and had just about made it halfway on a scarf for Court's Christmas gift when Jerry knocked on the trailer door. He peeked his head in, but his eyes did not meet mine as he said, "I was just checking e-mail. There's an urgent message for you. Your mother left a number. A hospital in L.A." At the nearest phone booth, I stared at hardened lumps of chewing gum and kicked the empty plastic phone-book holder, watching it swing on its large metal ring, as I waited on hold. When my mother came to the phone, her voice was oddly calm as she told me Court had been in an accident. I remember nothing from the drive to the airport except that I kept the needle at exactly 55, and a deer stared at me from the side of the road, which I took as a portent. I just didn't know of what. I was in my mother's kitchen by nine o'clock the next morning, California time, to learn my brother had died during the night of complications from a fall while rock climbing.

MY ROOM HAS GONE UNUSED ALL SUMMER, EARL TOLD ME when he settled my bags on the floor and opened the window, and even after I unpack, finding a drawer of nails in the dresser and one with bolts in the nightstand, it's still stuffy and warm. Outside, the sun has sunk behind the hills, but I can see the outline of the buildings just ahead as I cross through a field of dust and the rusted, dented metal of old pots and pans, bed springs, what looks like a bear trap. I step up on the boardwalk of the old telegraph office, the coffin maker's, the general store. Inside the coffin shop, tall caskets line the walls. One rests on two sawhorses, as if left by someone who intended to return the next day. The general store is locked. I sit on the edge of the boardwalk and pull my knees to my chest, look up. There will be no moon tonight, but the sky still holds enough blue to keep it distinct from the black hills, and when I feel the push of air against my face from beating wings, I turn to see the silhouettes of bats dipping out of the broken window above the coffin shop.

THE GRIEF AFTER COURT DIED WAS ENORMOUS, EXHAUSTING. It hung over every moment and insinuated itself in places that used to be free of emotion—waiting in line at the A & P, detaching the nozzle from the tank at a self-serve station, standing at a counter of the local post office to stick stamps onto envelopes, and driving to work. I live twenty minutes from my office along a busy road, and as I reached the corner where a stand of pines grows, just where the road begins to climb the hill toward Yankee Bank, as I eased up on the gas and downshifted, I'd be remembering how, one Saturday in the high school parking lot, Court had me turn up and down the rows of empty parking places while he repeated "Accelerate out of a turn," pushing his right hand through the air in the kind of smooth movement my two feet, jumping between three pedals, were supposed to get the car to make. I'd be thinking how, that November morning, I missed saying good-bye to him by three hours, so that by the time I reached the Yankee Bank, I'd be trying to figure out where I was over the country when he died, but deciding it was Kansas provided no detail, no relief, to the flat memory of that plane ride. I always kept driving, although once I pounded so hard on the steering wheel I bruised my fists.

Last Friday, Jerry brought a fax, stained with mayonnaise and a curl of shredded lettuce from his sandwich, over to my desk, where I was inputting plot points into the computer, and asked me if I'd ever heard of Bodie, California. "Found obsidian scatter there," he said. "Sounds like a chipping site. Parks says they need somebody to come take a look. Could be something, could be nothing. Why don't you go? You know the terrain."

"Where is it?"

"Near Bridgeport, says here. Mono County."

"The Eastern Sierra," I said. I didn't remind him California is the second largest state in the continental U.S. I didn't tell him I'd never been north of Santa Barbara or east of San Bernardino. I thought how there was nothing of Court in Connecticut except the crowded contents of my own brain, how, suddenly, I needed to be in California, where the ocean lies to the west, so the sun can set into it, the way—he used to say—it's supposed to.

MOST OF THE LIGHTS FROM THE FOUR RANGERS' CABINS ARE square, bright yellow, but some show a cone of white glare from the lamps over front doors or a multicolored flashing from a TV. Each lit house contains a world, a domestic place, yet there is a fragility in the way they are clustered together, surrounded by darkness, as if the lights had been poured into a bowl.

I push off from the boardwalk and walk toward the Cobodys. A beam of light jumps onto the road next to me, looming ahead to climb the peeling wood of the nearest abandoned cabin, and I hear men's voices, then a woman's, laughter.

"Hello," I call out, turning around, and the beam moves left and right until it shines in my eyes, then drops to my feet.

"It's Holly," one voice states, and then another, also male but with a lift of what—once I see it's Craig—I hear as enthusiasm, "Holly! Hey, how are you settling in?" And then they are in front of me: Craig, Dan, and a woman with long dark hair over one side of her pale, delicate face. Her eyelashes are long, and freckles sweep across her nose, the tops of her cheeks. She is pretty in the way of a woman who never wears make-up.

"I went out for a walk," I say, "but it got dark awfully fast."

"Happens up here," the woman says. "Eighty-four hundred feet."

"Next time," Dan says, "bring a flashlight." He swings the dual-beam lantern in his hand, illuminating the field of rust I walked through earlier in an wobbly arc.

"We'll walk you back," Craig says.

"Thanks," I say, "but I think I'm okay." I lift my hand and point ahead of me. Craig, smiling, turns my finger to point to my left. "You're at Earl's, right? We'll walk you." I smile, and as we move on, I fall behind Craig and Dan and the lantern light, to walk beside the woman. "We haven't met," I say.

I can't tell if she looks at me or not. "I'm Suzanne."

"I'm Holly."

Craig turns around to walk backwards. "Holly the archeologist. All the way from Massachusetts."

"Connecticut."

"Connecticut—to check out our bluff."

Dan has slowed, too, and we walk four abreast. I can see Suzanne's face again, a slight frown. "Don't we have archeologists in California?" she asks.

"Suzanne's our welcome wagon," Craig says. "But she's still in training."

Dan hoots, and Suzanne lifts her foot, kicks the back of Craig's thighs. The three of them lean into each other, laughing. They are friends, I see, good friends. Familiar sadness climbs into my chest

"My company has a contract with the Parks department," I say.

"It's a long way to come," she says.

Dan throws the beam of the lantern to make a circle: dark sky, curling tin roof, boarded window, dirt road, broken window, crumbled chimney, dark sky. The bright white beam bleaches the dirt and grasses and wood of the subtle coloring they held in daylight. Dan stops swinging the lamp when it shows a brick chimney, neatly shingled roof, lighted window guarded by rucked curtain, small sign on which someone has neatly painted Ranger's Residence. "Here you are," he announces. "Home safely, thanks to Bodie's finest escort team." He and Craig bow. Suzanne smiles and flips her hair over her shoulder. Craig, straightening, raises his eyebrows. "Hey, it's still early. If you're not too bushed, why don't you join us? We're just going to watch a video."

"Our nightly ritual," Dan says. "After the sunset doobie above the graveyard."

Ah. The laughter, the swinging lantern. Another rush of longing for Court, with whom I used to lie on the back lawn after our mother had gone to bed, mowed grass prickly under my bare legs, on nights of the full moon. It started when I was in seventh grade and he was taking astronomy as his first high-school elective, but we made it a monthly habit, talk about planetary placement and gravitational pull giving way, as we grew older, to confessions about crushes and fumbling dates and then to wowed stoned silence at the full moon rising over the neighbors' roofs and street lights to hang above us in the sky. Sometimes we'd hold hands, and I'd feel in the bones of his hand the only thing keeping me pinned to the orbiting earth.

"Oh thanks," I say, "but I'm pretty beat. The altitude. And I have a lot of work to do tomorrow." But as I turn away, I hear myself say, "It is a long way from Connecticut, but I wanted to come back to California. I grew up here."

And then I tell them—as I do more and more these days upon meeting people, because it is intrinsic to any introduction, as much a part of my identity as my name—about Court's death. Dan kicks the dirt. Craig says nothing, but I stare at his chest, suddenly wanting to put my head there.

"Dangerous stuff, rock climbing," Suzanne says, shaking her head. "You really take a risk. You have to be so careful."

"He was careful," I say, although I don't know this for sure.

She looks up, eyebrows lifted. "Of course." A placating smile. "I didn't mean he wasn't. I meant it's risky—even for those who are careful."

"Good night," I say, and turn my back to them, go inside. In the living room, the fish tank glows, its filter gurgles. I can hear the TV from down the hall. Back in my narrow room, cooler now, I take out the photo I keep in my wallet of Court and me as children, frowning in matching blue-and-white sailor suits, squinting into the sunlight behind our mother's camera. I reach into the dresser drawer, grab a handful of nails, push them through the photo into the wall until the pads of my fingertips bleed.

IN THE MORNING, THE STREETS OF BODIE ARE TRANSFORMED by sunshine. The town's forlorn presence is gone, replaced by a sense of expanse, a dry dusty smell that is almost sweet. It is only eight-thirty, but I have slathered sunblock over every exposed inch of skin.

The site is worse than I expected. Whatever integrity might have been here once has been undermined by rusty nails, broken glass on which the tatters of a beer label still cling, shredded cigarette filters. I anchor Ziploc bags with weights and walk around the small yellow flags marking where the scatter was found, plot the site on a sheet of grid paper. The ground is too hard to use the screens I brought, so I skim it with my flattened hand, the surface beneath the dust still cool, pleasing against my sore fingertips.

Earl told me there is a spring up here, but I am unconvinced of human habitation in these hills prior to the discovery of gold. It's too remote, too bleak. People passed through, most likely, or someone from Bodie found the obsidian elsewhere and brought it here. If this was a chipping site, there'd be signs of tools, maybe even bone fragment. I am beginning to think this is a waste of time, of money. I am thinking fondly of green trees, of thick lawn beneath the soles of my feet. I am remembering standing in front of an air conditioner, lifting my blouse over the vent when no one else is in the room.

My fingers hit something, something harder than dirt, and I reach for a brush. It is rock, rounded at the edge and buried at an angle. Ground rock would make sense if there is a spring nearby. The sun is almost straight overhead. I press a finger to my bare knee and release it. A white mark rises, then fades. I check that nothing will blow away, and walk down to town.

I go the wrong way off Main, finding myself at a dead end with a rusted model T chassis and a pile of neatly chopped and stacked wood, and turn around, almost collide with Craig. His face is so close I see the bleached hairs growing straight up between his eyebrows, the pores on the side of his nose. His bottom lip is puffier than the top lip, with a crease in the middle as if quilted. I draw back. He smiles, touches my forearm with his hand. "Hey."

I imagine sunscreen running off my face in rivulets, skin chalky with dust, hair tangled and askew. I have been pushing it back with the heel of my hand all morning. "Hi."

"Holly," he says. His voice is soft and slow, and I cannot take my eyes off his mouth. I have not felt this in a long time.

"Craig." I smile. And then I start blathering—about my morning, about the mess I found, the litter of glass, the cigarette butt, about the obsidian, about what I think might be ground rock. Suzanne walks up as I'm talking, and I tell her that I was just asking Craig if he knows where the spring is.

"I know where it was three months ago," he says.

"But that's not necessarily the same place it was last year," Suzanne says. "Or a hundred years ago."

I know that.

"I'll take you up there, show you," Craig tells me.

"Okay," I say. "Let's go."

He cocks his head, and when his eyes narrow, his mouth opens so slowly the dry skin of his lips pulls apart along a thin line. I imagine those lips sticking briefly to mine, a dry brush of a kiss before tasting his tongue. I don't even know this man.

"Holly," he says, his use of my name now formal as he stands back. "It's too hot. You just got here. Have a big lunch. Drink a lot of water. Take a nap. We'll go up later, when it's cooler." His eyes are focused on something behind me, and his attitude is fraternal, not sexual. I have had too much sun.

I eat lunch with Earl and Dawn, and take a nap and write a letter to my mother, and then, after dinner, Craig and I climb back up to the bluff. He rips his shirt bending over barbed wire outside the abandoned mine, and finds the spring after walking around a large white outcropping. He shows me the thin stream that comes up through split rock, tinting it green and wetting the finger I press to the spot.

I DON'T KNOW WHERE I AM. I OPEN MY EYES SUDDENLY ON dark wooden walls, mouth dry and heart pounding at the sight of Court still fixed on the backs of my eyelids—falling straight down, hurtling past sheer gray granite, close enough to touch but he can't because he is falling too fast, falling endlessly. My hands reach out and grab the resistant nap of the blue blanket, its synthetic fuzz tipped in white like bear fur. Over its folds at my feet, a slice of sunlight narrows and widens as the air from the open window sucks the shade against the frame and then billows it into the room again.

My earliest memories are of pausing and trembling with interrupted childhood energy while Court ran ahead to make sure the mean dog was behind the fence or climbed up a tree first to check for loose branches. He took his role as older brother seriously, once even beating up two sixth-graders who'd made fun of my shiny plastic rain hat when I stepped off the school bus. I moved back east for college, and stayed. Court was a confirmed Californian, skiing and rock climbing and mountain biking and, every summer, just after the passes opened, hiking in Tuolumne Meadows, where he woke once to an eagle soaring above his tent and splashed in creeks that had ten minutes earlier been snow.

We talked weekly on the phone, still discussing our love lives. Our parents had split when we were eight and ten, and our skittishness expressed itself differently. Court played the aloof male, stringing several women along at once. "She's a lot of fun," he'd often say, "but not a taker." By that he meant not gifts or sex, but someone who would "take"—"you know," he'd say, "like fixative." I clung and clung even when I knew the guy was all wrong for me. I'd make excuses to my girlfriends, and to myself—but to my brother, I couldn't lie. He was the only one I told that they all left me.

EARL TELLS ME IT IS BODIE TRADITION ON MONDAY NIGHTS to gather outside the general store, open the doors, plug a stereo into the generator behind the counter, and have a party. So after dinner I take a bath and put on the only dress I brought. I watch myself draw brown lines under each eye and smudge them with my little finger, pull my hair back into a barrette and loosen a few strands in front. I look into my own eyes and then away, remembering the dream that woke me this morning and kept me motionless on the bed, watching the sunlight move across the floor. As I lean toward the mirror now, I feel loneliness deep in my belly, like an arrow that quivers after stabbing its target, but I sweep it over with the brush of a mascara wand, a push of my fingers through my eyebrows. My eyes are shining, my cheeks flushed. I think of Craig, and catch myself smiling.

No one's there yet, but the doors to the general store are open, a generator propped against the wall under the front window, its cord neatly coiled like a snake with the plug for a head. The floorboards give under my steps. Faded foodstuff boxes and grain bags line the tops of shelves. Colored glass jars with stoppers decorate the wooden countertops. Rounded-glass display cases show old spectacles with wire rims, binoculars, tortoise-shell combs and lace handkerchiefs and elaborately painted Japanese fans displayed on pale pink satin. Most of these items, the typed index card reads, along with the tufted sofas and chairs in the back of the room, were salvaged from a bordello in the 1892 fire. Bodie may have been the bad town of the West, but this bordello had higher standards than one might think. I touch the fringe of a lamp, and its yellow material is cool and soft between my fingers: silk. The maroon fabric of the shade is watermarked in moiré. A pleasant breeze comes through the open double doors and stirs my skirt. The light has faded, and the setting sun shines copper against the old barn across the road. Dust spins slowly through the air.

On top of the next case is a box of postcards, "$2 each," according to the sign propped up at the end of the box. Many of these are full-color representations of Bodie today: its blue mining buildings up along the slope of the bluff, a close-up of the vault whose bank burned around it in 1932, views of Samuel Godby's coffin shop, of the brick courthouse, of the Manner house, Bodie's best preserved house (I know from earlier today, when I walked through on peeling linoleum to see metal chairs pushed back from a wooden table, sagging bedsprings beneath a ripped and chewed mattress, a washboard and bucket, and above it all, hanging from the corners of the ceiling, the intricate crochet of cobwebs). My fingers move desultorily through the postcards, then stop. Toward the back are some cards that have been made from old photographs, photographs displayed on the wall behind the counter. Genuine Bodie residents. I pull out one of three men in front of the courthouse, and carry it to the window to look at it in the fading light. Two lawmen wearing silver stars stand on either side of a man who the blurb on the back tells me is Tom Adams, believed by many to be the legendary Badman from Bodie, arrested at last by Sheriff Pete Harrison and his deputy.

These men look tough, grim, black eyes flat as stones. I don't like looking at them, but I can't look away. Then I know what they remind me of: the wax museum I visited as a child. Court and I walked through together, and he told me that the eyes were real; they'd been cut out from people in hospitals before they died. I believed him, because I always believed him. "Watch," he whispered, as we moved past one display, "their eyes will follow you. Stay close." I was thrilled with fear and his protectiveness as he followed me into each new gallery, saying I'd be safer going first. Then, right before the exit, he tickled me. I screamed, hitting him, laughing with relief to be away from those wax statues' eyes, which looked both full of mystery and completely empty.

AT THE PARTY, CRAIG STANDS NEXT TO ME, AND WHILE WE don't touch, the space between us feels charged, like two magnets placed end to end. We talk about driving across the country, about camping along rivers, about childhood vacations and summer camp. He asks me if I've had any more luck at the site, and pulls the tail of his shirt from his pants, reminds me of the hazards of barbed wire. Through the rip in the fabric, his skin is pale.

When Willie Nelson plays from the speakers, we dance. I sway my hips and step back, away, our arms outstretched; I fit under his arm and my steps fall in with his as they take me back to him. His grip is secure and relaxed. We look at each other. We smile. Earl comes up at the end of the dance, says there are people I need to meet, and I follow him, meet the others, shake hands. I fall into conversation with a year-round ranger, and when I look back to the dancers, the cold glass of a beer bottle against my lips, the music has changed. Craig is dancing with Suzanne, her long black hair swinging in a curtain when she turns her head, lifts her face to his, and smiles. She looks a little out of breath. I can't see Craig's face, only the flat planes of his back as he leads her in a two-step.

We do not kiss until we are out of sight of the others. He is walking me home. Earl and Dawn left a long time ago, but I know the back door will be open. With ten people living here and a gate that closes at seven, there is no security problem. It is another difference from Connecticut, another thing that seems unreal. At the back door, Craig lifts his arm against the jamb, his shadow looming from the lamp above the door. After several minutes, I open the door just enough to kill the light and then close it again, and we run hand in hand to the house he shares with Dan and two other men, to his room down the hall from the others. He shuts the door, and we turn to each other, pull off each other's clothes while we kiss. In bed I kneel astride him, take from his hand the condom he's pulled from a bureau drawer and unwrap it, roll it on. It's dark in the room, but I can see enough to know he's looking up at me, surprised by my forthrightness. I am, too—amazed, actually, at my body that knows exactly what it wants and plows over the grief to get it.

IN THE COBODY KITCHEN, QUIET EXCEPT FOR THE BREATHY puff and gurgle of Mr. Coffee, I measure, label, and bag the dust and chips I've found in two days, write up my notes, make a neater graph. If I can get this faxed to Jerry by noon Connecticut time, he should be able to get back to me by the end of the day. I still feel Craig's arms around me, but I do not indulge in my usual day-after musings about weddings, children's names, or where we will build our first house. I wonder if this is what Court meant when, after I asked him once how he could sleep so easily with women he hardly knew, how it could mean nothing, he told me, "It doesn't mean nothing, it just doesn't mean everything."

At the edge of the parking lot, my rental car glares blue in the sun. I haven't been up here since arriving on Saturday, and have forgotten how the graveyard lies across the road leading out of the park, adjacent to the laborers' camp, as if the dead, like the Chinese, could be kept forever foreign, forever designated to one role.

I cross the road, step in through the gate, stop short. I know that a squared fence and headstones are not requisites to burial ground. The dead are under every footstep, in one way or another. I have been trained to know this, and to look past it. Yet I back out quickly, close the gate, edge along the fence to lean over and peer at a headstone, smaller than the two next to it and marked like its neighbor with only a first name and dates. A child of six months next to her three-year-old brother. To the third headstone, belonging to Abigail, aged twenty-five, is added a last name and the words "Devoted wife and mother," but there is no man buried with them, no husband and father to complete the family. Did he leave Bodie and his sorrow behind? A mourner at these fresh graves would have seen before him the same bleak hills I see now. He could have carried this view in his memory the rest of his life. He could have pulled it out like a snapshot, saying to himself, *There, they are there*, and closed his grief around one particular place.

We don't know quite how Court fell. He had a crushed pelvis and so many broken bones that the rescue crew who brought him out said his ropes must have failed. I wonder if he felt the ropes give, if he knew what was happening, if his last moment was one of fear—or, knowing Court, one of disgust. I can imagine this—disgust at fallible ropes, disgust even at himself, and then I can go no further, no further than the thought that there is no marker where he fell, no headstone beneath which he lies. He was cremated, and we scattered his ashes from a rented plane above Tuolumne Meadows, a place I cannot picture except from 14,000 feet, a height at which it was impossible to see where they landed.

On the dull packed dirt of Abigail's grave, there is a spot from where shafts of light still radiate after I blink, a glistening of something bright. I push through the gate, crouch down to get a better look, an angle with less glare. I know what it is before I pick it up, before I touch the tiny crescents beveled like fish scales along its edges, the sharp tip, the blunt end. Its weight feels like a feather's in my palm. This graveyard has been here over a hundred years. There have been thirty-foot drifts of snow over this land, dust storms that made Earl and Dawn seal their windows with wet paper towels, tourists kicking and stirring up dirt with their boots, their Reeboks, their Teva sandals. An obsidian arrowhead can't have been here all this time, intact, lying on top of the dirt as if dropped this morning. It is glossy smooth, black beyond any black I've ever seen, a black that jumps the sunlight back into my eyes. I pocket the arrowhead, and before standing up, sweep my fingers through the dirt where it had lain.

CRAIG FINDS ME ON MY WAY DOWN FROM THE BLUFF. I'VE BEEN at the site since ten, when I returned from sending the fax, fortified by more coffee and a huge Danish from town, and am craving a nap when hands cup my shoulders from behind, turn me to press my face into a neck scratchy with stubble and smelling of Bodie's dry dust. We step back into the lean-to of shade against the nearest building to murmur and kiss before walking to his place. In his room, I pick up his shirt from the back of a chair, where it landed the night before. "This is the one with the rip."

His arms go around my waist as he pulls me to him, props his chin on my shoulder. "Uh-huh."

"You have a needle and thread? I'll fix it."

He's kissing my neck, one hand finding its way beneath my shirt, where it is cold against my skin. "You don't need to do that."

"I want to." I move away from him to sit on the bed, pulling the shirt onto my lap. The rip is off the seam, but straight and neat, about two inches long. "It'll only take five minutes."

He looks puzzled, but smiles his slow, easy smile, one corner of his mouth pulling up before the other. "Promise?" He reaches for a dopp kit on the bureau, fumbles inside, hands me a hotel sewing packet.

He watches as I mend the shirt, lying on his side and tracing circles on my bare knee. Sunshine streams through the window beneath the curtains. I push the needle through the soft fabric, watching the thread pull the two edges together in the blindstitch I learned in seventh grade Home Ec. I do not look up until I am finished, biting the thread off the knot I have just tied, so that by the time I see the desire on his face, I am steadied by my own stitching, as rhythmic as breathing, and ready.

JERRY CALLS AS I'M DOING THE DINNER DISHES AT EARL AND Dawn's. He thanks me for the fax and asks if I've found anything new since sending it, since the four words I had written before seeing Abigail's grave, the four words I did not change: *No new obsidian found.*

"No," I say, fingering the small object in my pocket. "Nothing." I know what I'm doing, going against every professional instinct I've ever had, every rule I've been taught. I cannot tell Jerry what I found, what I took, because he would expect me to dig there, too, and I would refuse.

"Okay," he says. "Keep going. You've only been there a few days. I'll talk to Parks, get back to you." He tells me they've had thunderstorms every day since I left, that the trees outside his office window are dripping heavily with rain. I close my eyes, see green so thick I can breathe it.

ON OUR THIRD NIGHT TOGETHER, WHEN CRAIG AND I GO into Bridgeport for dinner, a fax is waiting for me at the grocery store. Jerry says the Parks Department wants a full and thorough report. They believe the ground rock is an encouraging sign, and he agrees. They want me to enlarge the site at the bluff, dig further. I'm not surprised. "Looks like I'll be here another week or two," I say to Craig. "They're not granting mining rights anytime soon."

"Too bad for Earl," he says, brushing my hair back from my forehead. "But I'm glad. Mono's only a forty-minute drive, and I'm off every weekend."

I've known since the party that his regular job is in Mono Lake, that he's been in Bodie only for July, but I smile, say nothing. It's not until we're at the restaurant, after we've eaten, that he says he's going back the next day. My hand stops fingering the linen napkin next to my plate.

He covers my hand with his. "I just found out. I wish I didn't have to go."

The seed of a thought has taken root, is growing. He has a long-term girlfriend in Mono, a fiancée, a wife. For the first time in my life, these possibilities are promising, and I wonder if he hears this in my voice when I ask, "Are you involved with anybody?"

He nudges my hand so our palms touch and spreads my fingers with his, moving against the skin along the sides. "Well, there's this one woman, a really sweet archeologist, in fact she's sitting right here." He raises my hand to his lips, which I brush with my thumb and then stop. "I've never met anyone like you, Holly."

"There must be someone in your life."

He shakes his head, makes a small frown. "Not in a long time. Suzanne and I slept together a few times back in April, but that doesn't count."

"Suzanne?"

"Yeah. We'd gotten together a few years back, when she was at Mono, too. We've always been friends. You know how these things can happen."

"Uh-huh. Like what happened with me." My voice is calm. He leans forward quickly. "No, not at all. Holly." I pull my hand away to make room for the busboy to clear the plates. Craig says, "Don't think that. What happened with you was wonderful, a wonderful surprise." He rubs a finger along my cheek, and I close my eyes even as I lean into his touch, to see an arm around his back that isn't mine, long strands of black hair against his chest, to hear my brother's words. "Not a taker, Holly, not a taker."

OUTSIDE, WE LEAN AGAINST HIS TRUCK FOR A LONG TIME. HIS arms are tight around my shoulders and his thighs press against mine, but I feel suspended, weightless, as I watch the traffic signal sway above the road. The light changes, and campers and cars accelerate through the intersection. Some drivers will pass the turn-off to Bodie without knowing it's there, just as tourists walked its streets today without imagining those of us who drove out after them to bolt the gate, those of us who will return tomorrow to bend alone over the dust and under the bowl of blue sky and heat.

I turn my head and look past Craig's shoulder at the windows of the Bridgeport Inn, glowing with a coziness that is now out of reach, and when he kisses the top of my head I feel his lips as if already in the past. There is a slight wind from the west, and it blows my hair into my mouth. The Sawtooths are jagged black against the sunset, and I imagine I can see to Yosemite on the other side, and to a climber who scales a face he was never meant to climb, who reaches the top, who does not fall.

Bees for Honey

THE MCDONOUGH PLACE WAS RIGHT ACROSS THE ROAD FROM ours. A circle of green fields spread out around the two houses like an apron, the road a gray ribbon running east into town and west to the coast. The horizon, where the blurry edge of a field or a line of trees met the sky, was unimaginably far. The traffic on our road whispered to me of places whose names I knew from green interstate on-ramp signs, but at nine I had no interest in listening. A few years later, a new freeway link would be built between the interstate and the coast highway, cutting in half the drive to the fishing towns and beach resorts. It would leave us the schoolbus and tractors and pickups, and take away my sense of home as a place of any significance or self-sufficiency.

I was not the child of farmers. We had a small strawberry crop so my father, a dentist, had something to talk about with his patients. Our fields were leased to produce companies, and although from the road our property looked as immense as the

McDonoughs', it ended at the scraggly cypress windbreak for my mother's rose beds. The McDonoughs' land extended behind their house as far as the river, a mile south, and at least a mile on either side. Mr. McDonough and his two sons, Kevin and Joey, farmed and raised bees. At school, I'd heard Kevin McDonough brag about his father's ranch in terms of acres of lettuce, rows of artichokes, and tens of thousands of bees.

Merrill McDonough was my age but in second grade, where her mussed blond head stuck up a neck higher than the heads of the seven-year-olds in a circle on the carpet for story time. She walked on the balls of her feet and wore gauzy dresses whose sashes and bows made her look like she was on her way to a birthday party. I'd heard my mother say, Really, what could you expect?: Merrill's mother bought her the dresses but never told her they were wrong for everyday. And Merrill herself, how could she know what was appropriate? At recess, the meaner boys would circle around her, making buzzing noises. Merrill always smiled when she saw me coming, and the hand she held out to mine was often sticky with honey.

Warm weekends, my mother sat outside reading a magazine, her face protected by a yellow cotton hat; my father worked, voices from radio talk shows calling from his office's open door. When the driveway got too hot for bare feet, Merrill and I made a shade fort of blankets draped over my mother's patio furniture, accessible only by belly-crawl. Enough sun came through the fabric to fleck our tented world, but it was mostly shadowy and cool. I'd long ago given up blocks at school, but with Merrill I would use my old wooden ones to make walls and furniture for our tent. Merrill sat with her doll, combing out her hair with a twig. When our faces were flushed and moist under the blanket and we were thirsty for fresh air, we'd stand up at the same time and shriek with glee as our privacy collapsed around us.

One afternoon as I built a precariously balanced pyramid of the smooth blond blocks, Merrill stopped combing to watch, put her doll down, and reached for the crowning block and set it down again on the top of the pyramid, gently, with a smile, and turned back to her doll. There was no reason to speak.

THE MCDONOUGH HOUSE AND OURS WERE TWINS, SQUAT, one-story ranch-style houses built by two brothers back in the fifties. The yellow house with its small windows set high had always been the first thing I saw in the morning when I raised my window shades. Sometimes, late at night, I woke to the sound of a pickup pulling up, braking, turning off. Kneeling on my bed, I inched the shade aside to watch Mr. McDonough hop down from the cab, slam the door, and when after a minute the light in their kitchen window went on, I watched as he stood at the stove reheating dinner and then ate standing: ducking his head, forking up food. I imagined bacon and eggs, hamburger and chopped onions and tomato sauce, grilled cheese sandwiches, the private clatter of heavy black saucepans, always careful to keep my face out of the sliver between shade and window. When he turned to put the dishes in the sink, I let go of the shade and felt the pulse at the side of my neck as I imagined him seeing the shade sway, wondering why. He was big and his heavy hands were caked with dirt and he had a gruff, low voice that hoarsened when he yelled at Joey once for climbing on an idling backhoe. I spied on aching knees until he left the kitchen as opaque and dark as the rest of their house. When I walked out our front door in the morning, Mr. McDonough and his truck would already have left for the fields, and the kitchen window would be blank and benign.

The first of the artichokes were ready in October. The picking started at the far end of the fields, so Merrill and I stayed close to the road while we waited for the school bus. The chokes themselves grew at the base of the plant, little knobs that sprung out, too pliable to break easily when young. Ripe, the bulb snapped cleanly from its stalk, outside leaves tightly bound and tipped with small sharp points. On cold mornings when fog lay low along the ground, we picked artichokes and held them in our sweaters like dolls. Other times, we pulled off the outside leaves with fast, downward tugs as a bitter, musty smell escaped. We gripped and yanked the wrinkled leaves in a race to reach the fuzzy choke. Uncooked, it was moist and soft, inseparable from the heart below, as yellow as the discarded inner leaves at our feet. Holding the stalks like handles, we brought the fragrant chokes to our noses as if they were powder puffs. The artichokes were planted in lines so straight my eyes flicked from one to the next as if they were fence slats when I rode by in a car or bus, but here in the field, it seemed Merrill and I were at the center of an endless spiral as we bent and pulled and snapped and tossed. Skipping among the artichokes took us across and between precise and intentional rows, but I felt surrounded by random splendor.

I'D RECENTLY STARTED RIDING MY BIKE TO SCHOOL, AND WAS circling the playground before riding home when I saw girls from my class gathered by the bus stop. I heard laughter and felt lifted by possibilities. Lisa had spoken to me that day in library hour, and she'd let me have *The Borrowers* that she'd just finished. "Be friendly," my mother always said. "Smile and be yourself and people will like you." Maybe it really was that simple.

As I got closer, I saw they made a tight knot whose center was Merrill. Belinda, leaning forward, her weight on one foot and hand on the other hip, was slowly lifting Merrill's hair from the back of her neck. She dropped it suddenly, as if she realized too late she was touching something she didn't want to, and the others laughed. It was not the kind of laughter my mother had talked about. Catie pointed at Merrill's patent leather shoes. "Where's the party?"

"Better comb your bird's nest before the party."

"Why didn't you invite us to your party, Merrill? It's not nice to leave people out."

"Where's your present? It's rude to go without a present!"

"Are you going to play pin-the-tail-on-the-donkey?"

Merrill was laughing, too, looking from one face to another. I dropped my bike and walked over. Catie stepped back. "Mollie. Are you invited to Merrill's party?"

I walked into the knot and grabbed Merrill's hand. "Come on. They're laughing at you."

I could feel three sets of eyes on me as I pulled Merrill away. I picked up my bike and headed with it and Merrill off the playground. Behind us was silence, and then one of them yelled, "Have fun at the party!"

I woke up the next morning tasting metal. When my mother walked in my room to snap up the window shades, I felt like throwing up. I cleared my throat repeatedly at the breakfast table, hunched over my bowl, and pushed my cereal around with a spoon.

"What's wrong, Mollie? Don't you feel well?"

My eyes did not meet hers. "My stomach feels funny."

Her palm on my forehead was moist from the sponge she'd been using to wipe the counter. "You don't have a fever. You'll feel better once you get to school."

I tried again when I left the house, curling the toe of my sneaker to rub out an imaginary stain on the front step, and holding my stomach with my hands. "Go on," she said. "Have a good day, off you go," and with a kiss on my head and a firm hand between my shoulder blades, she sent me off.

It seemed to me my parents lived in a cocoon: my father with his patients who had to pay him and be polite, his office-supply catalogues, the occasional out-of-town conference; my mother with her heirloom roses and paintings and clothes—short slim pants and big, baggy shirts—that none of the other mothers wore. Danger was everywhere. I didn't understand how they could fail to see it.

But in homeroom Belinda smiled at me and Lisa asked me if I was liking *The Borrowers*, and when they made room for me on the turning bar at recess, I asked if they wanted to come over to my house some time.

THE MEN WORKED UNTIL AFTER I GOT HOME FROM SCHOOL, but when I went outside after supper, the lowering sun reflected off fields empty of both man and machine. The traffic on the road had ceased and the pinpricks of light from other houses, three miles away, seemed as distant as stars. Birds called from the fields and from my mother's garden; marsh hawks swung low and dipped suddenly to catch mice and lizards. Merrill and Kevin and I played outside in the magic twilight, in deepening shadows, in the darkness that slid so seamlessly over us that I saw better at this hour than at midday when I had to squint. The sun sank at the end of the bladelike road, catching in glints and flashes the chrome of my bicycle, the zipper on Kevin's jacket, Merrill's glossy shoes. We kept inside boundaries made by the row of cypresses, the edges of driveways, the two rickety mailboxes where the school bus stopped. The lights from our houses spilled onto shrubs and pavement and wheelbarrows. The McDonoughs' front windows were either dark or curtained, but my parents were visible from the waist up, side by side, as they stood at the sink washing and drying the dishes.

We counted to one hundred if Merrill was hiding, and stuck an elbow or a foot out if she was seeking. One night, Merrill picked the same hiding place four times in a row, returning to an old oak stump at the edge of the McDonoughs' front yard. Pedaling my way back to Merrill with an especially small acorn or a perfect round striped wishing rock, I almost ran my bicycle into the stump before I saw her, in the darkness right in front of me. My mother's voice called out its sing-song "Mol-lie-it's-dark." I placed my collected treasure in Merrill's lap and yelled into the air, "I got to go!" I dropped my bicycle at the edge of the driveway and went inside, where the electric light in our front hall stunned me. Standing at the kitchen sink to pour a glass of water, I marveled at the black square of window in front of me. It didn't seem possible that I'd just been out in that.

Sometimes Merrill ran outside with a spoon in her mouth. She sat on the stump and sucked on the spoon. If she started to run or jump, her brother took the spoon away from her. I had been in the McDonough kitchen enough to know there was always honey on the table, lids were always crusty and tacky and didn't screw on right, smudges streaked the kitchen table, and the straw trivet under the jar was circled with dark stains.

I liked Merrill's house. We could play there all afternoon and not see another person, so different from my house, where my mother walked through, telling us to go outside in the fresh air and sunshine, or tuned her radio to Jazz 99 while she cooked or painted, and the phone rang for my father, and where I had to close the door to my room for privacy. At the McDonoughs', the deep pile rug absorbed the noise of our footsteps, and Merrill's mother spent her time in the bedroom, behind a door that was ajar just enough to let the blue glow and low murmur of a television spill out as a sign of life within.

Merrill and I were having bananas and milk, taking a break from cutting out paper dolls, when Mr. McDonough came in, the screen door banging behind him. I stiffened. I stared at the unlidded honey jar with the spoon sticking out of it, and mumbled something when he greeted me: "Hello, Mollie."

"Hey ya, Merry honey." He reached out his hand and touched the top of Merrill's blond head. A look of softness came over his craggy features, and he stroked her fine, tangled hair, his hand encompassing the whole dome of her skull. I imagined such a hand landing on my head, and I held my breath. But Merrill kept eating, her eyes on her bowl, in her slow and concentrated way, while Mr. McDonough's calloused hand gently brushed her hair. He looked up, toward the sink, and I saw his gaze land on the counter. His hand stopped on Merrill's head and he turned to me. Quietly and calmly, as he lifted a lock of her hair and rubbed it between two fingers, he said, "Mollie, you be sure to put that knife away." I nodded. Merrill had small dull scissors with rounded tips that we used for cutting out paper dolls. At home I used the heavy pointed ones from my mother's kitchen drawer. I didn't tell Mr. McDonough that Merrill had watched me slice one banana and then squirmed in her chair until I gave her the knife. She'd held it with both hands, like a saw, and cut neat, if uneven, slices.

One Sunday afternoon, when no one was working in the fields and Mr. McDonough had taken Kevin and Joey to an auction, Merrill led me to the back corner of the ranch, under the shade of the gum trees by the river. I knew the McDonoughs' fields as well as my own house, but I had been told my whole life to stay away from the apiary, especially after heavy rain or harvesting, which upset the bees. I'd seen Mr. McDonough and Joey on their way out here before, each wearing pants cinched at the ankles and a hat with a net that hung from the brim and disappeared into the neck of his long-sleeved shirt. I'd watched from a distance as they scraped honey off the frames while the bees swarmed around them in black clouds. But I'd never been this close, and I shivered as we left the field and were in the shade of the gum trees, where fallen seed pods poked through the thin rubber soles of my sneakers. I could see the gray boxes that housed ten comb frames each; there were six of them, stacked in twos, neatly, in a small clearing. There was a shed, too, with a heavy padlock on its door. I stopped and Merrill turned to me with her usual blank serenity. "Want honey."

I shook my head. "There's honey at home, Merrill. Lots of it."

"*I'm* not scared," she said, but I didn't walk any farther. She took a few steps closer to the boxes, and then stopped, looking back at me. I shook my head and she shrugged, just barely, and we turned our backs on the boxes and walked home through the fields.

BELINDA FINALLY ACCEPTED MY INVITATION, AND SHE AND Catie and Lisa rode bikes home with me one day. They stood behind me in our living room as I watched my mother pick up her purse and scarf. "You girls help yourselves to a snack if you want. Mollie, maybe you would like to serve the rest of last night's pie?" I nodded, but was thinking of the limited supply of Hostess cakes my mother bought each week for my school lunches and trying to remember how many were left.

"Thank you so much, Mrs. Kottke. You have such a lovely home."

My mother's smile twitched with an amusement I hoped the others didn't notice. "You're welcome, Belinda. Come over again soon and play." *Hurry up,* I silently begged, as I watched her pick up the car keys from the hook by the door.

"Bye, girls. I'll see you in a hour or so, Mollie."

I nodded. *Go.*

"Bye." A chorus raised against the closing door.

When it closed, I turned around. Catie was moving toward the front window. "*Play,*" she said. "Can I come over again and play?"

Lisa said, "Come on, you guys. We have to move fast."

"Okay, she's gone," Catie cried, and jumped back from the window to face me. "Are all your mom's pants floods, Mollie? Let's go look in her closet. I bet she has really dorky stuff."

"Shut up, Catie," Belinda yelled from the kitchen, where she stood at the open refrigerator door. "Didn't your mother ever teach you manners?"

Catie rolled her eyes, but her cheeks were pink.

"Mollie," Belinda began, closing the door, "can you keep a secret?"

"Sure. Do you want something to eat?"

She stepped back into the living room, closer to me. "We have one thing to take care of, and then we'll all play." She used the word neutrally, with no inflection.

"Okay."

"You know Kevin McDonough, right?"

I nodded.

"Last week him and his sister stole apricots from Catie's farm." Her voice was steady, a lesson in seduction.

We had played in the street every day before supper, I knew. But I chewed my lip, asked "When?"

Catie had moved to stand next to Belinda, and I saw her roll her eyes again. She and Lisa giggled. Belinda's eyes did not leave mine, and her voice was sweet when she said, "Thursday."

Merrill and Kevin had been in the street when my mother drove me home from chorus practice, like always. Catie's farm was on the other side of town. Merrill and Kevin could not have made it all the way there and back and still done

Kevin's chores in time. But at that moment, I would have given Belinda anything.

We took four eggs from the carton in the refrigerator, and Lisa and I followed Catie out the front door, while Belinda watched sentry from my bedroom window. One car passed, but with its out-of-state license plates it was nothing to worry about. We ran across the road and around the outside of the McDonoughs' house, crouching close to the camellia bushes planted along the foundation. The bedrooms were in back, facing the fields. I pointed to Kevin's room, but they wanted Merrill's, and we stopped beneath her open window. Lisa pushed two eggs at me, and I took them, threw them in, where they broke on the carpet next to Merrill's bed. Lisa threw one too and was reaching for the last when Catie turned around suddenly: "Hey!" Mr. McDonough's tractor was in the fields, heading home. Lisa dropped the fourth egg and we ran back to the street.

Back in my house, we fell on the living room carpet, and when I caught my breath, I suggested playing Twister or Trouble. Catie smirked and Belinda said, "Mollie, we have to go now. We'll see you at school tomorrow." I wanted to hear friendship in her voice, but I wasn't sure. The rest of the day and all evening I waited for a knock on the door from Mr. McDonough or maybe Joey, asking what I'd been doing that afternoon, or a question from my mother about the depleted carton of eggs, but neither came. The next morning I dawdled until I missed the bus and then convinced my mother I had a sore throat. By the time my father finished his morning appointments to come look at it, I felt much better.

THE HARVEST CONTINUED THROUGH NOVEMBER, BUT WITH the shorter days, Kevin and Merrill and I no longer played in the road after supper. At school, Belinda and Catie and Lisa made up reptile nicknames for each other—Belinda was Tuatara, Catie was Iguana, and Lisa was Horny Toad. Even Lisa's little sister, a first grader, was called Gecko. At night at home I looked through the *World Book Encyclopedia* for exotic reptile names, but they never asked me for one. More and more, I spent recess in the library, slouched in a corner where the bookshelves met the wall, reading.

The air went cold as soon as the sun sank behind trees, but it was still warm when I walked home from school. I was caught up in a jumping-rope game I'd watched on the playground, and was practicing the steps confidently, with no one to see. That morning, the fields had looked plucked clean and I'd thought the picking was done. The earth was fallow under my skipping feet, littered with bits of cut hay and seed pods, but when I looked up, I saw a big green harvester and men between me and the road. I'd have to walk along the far edge of the McDonoughs' fields, by the gum trees, to get around them. It wasn't far, and it looked nice and shady. The motor of the harvester hummed and men's low voices called out. They were headed away from me, and I kept to the line where the cloddy field met the hard, unplanted earth dappled in shadow from the tall gum trees. I could see the apiary shed up ahead through the trees and watched for the hives. As I neared the clearing, I saw them, gray boxes spread out on the ground.

Merrill walked among them, holding a glass jar. She gave no sign of seeing me. She placed the jar on the ground and pulled a frame from the nearest box and held it in both hands. Dark flecks rose from the frame and floated around Merrill's head like ashes. She propped the frame against the side of the box, and its surface moved, an alive brown carpet. She lifted another frame with her bare arms, the harsh electric sound whining louder as the flecks flew into dense hovering clumps. Underneath the sun-warmed fabric of my shirt, sweat tickled my skin.

I heard an engine and turned to see Mr. McDonough on a tractor; there was nowhere to hide, but he didn't seem to notice me, and when the tractor drew abreast of the clearing, he killed the engine and dropped down from the cab, stood still and stared, then pulled off his hat and squinted. His head cocked, and making a strange, low cry, he ran toward Merrill, unmoving near the box, her face uplifted, offering itself to the bees. She didn't see her father until he lifted her. His free arm swung in the air as he ran, and the other hand pressed Merrill's face into his shoulder. Her dress flew in the wind, the rumpled sash bannering out behind them. I did not breathe as I watched the bees, a dark stain against the bright sky, following her blond head and fluttering dress, the patent leather of her Mary Janes gleaming in the sun. Mr. McDonough didn't run back to the tractor but instead toward their house. The bees thinned out as he ran into the field, and I watched the mass of them turn back to their scattered gray boxes and frames.

I stepped on something as I backed farther into the field. Mr. McDonough's hat lay in a gutted row. I picked it up and walked to his tractor, reaching up to hoist myself onto the tire and place the hat on the seat. I jumped down, and when I landed in the dirt, I remembered that children were not allowed to climb on tractors. Nor were we supposed to go near the bees. I saw Mr. McDonough's frown and heard his gruff voice as if he were standing next to me, heavy boots on the cloddy field, and when I lifted my head and the vision fell away, another took its place like the next dealt card, that of Merrill, alone, cleaning broken eggs from her carpet.

RAIN GUSTED AGAINST MY BEDROOM WINDOW ALL NIGHT long, sucking the shades against the rattling glass and falling like thrown pebbles against the panes. Each time I started to fall asleep, I'd see Merrill's bare skin, her father's squint, his hand over her eyes, and I'd jerk awake again to stare at darkened walls. I'd pull back the shade and look outside. The McDonoughs' kitchen light stayed on all night, but no tall shape showed itself in the window.

The next morning huge puddles pocked our front path. The clouds had passed by the time I left for school, and the sun was coming out. Merrill was not on the bus, and I did not see her when I went outside for recess. When I stopped at her house on my way home, no one answered the door bell. The door was locked. My mother had graham crackers and a glass of milk waiting for me in our kitchen. I sat down.

"Honey, I have some bad news about the McDonoughs."

I stared at her.

"The McDonoughs lost their bees in last night's storm. A lot of them got away, and others drowned."

I picked up a graham cracker and bit off a corner, but couldn't swallow it. The dry piece sat on my tongue.

"Mr. McDonough was badly stung yesterday."

I looked down.

"Were you playing with Merrill yesterday afternoon?"

I shook my head.

"Well, she was out at the apiary." My mother lifted the empty Lazy Susan from the center of the table and brushed the crumbs from under it into a cupped hand. "She was alone at their house, or unsupervised"—I knew this was a reference to Mrs. McDonough—"and she wandered out there. Thank God he got to her when he did. As it is, she only got a few stings." She shook her head. "All those bees, and that poor, unknowing child."

"But she likes the bees. They don't hurt her. You don't know."

My mother turned from the sink, where she was dusting crumbs from her palms into the basin. "Do you know any more about this?"

"No." A wedge had come between my mother and me on those mornings when I'd pleaded sick, and it widened now. "She wasn't at school today."

"I know." My mother's face softened. "She may not go back. The McDonoughs have decided that Merrill needs more supervision, a special school where teachers are trained to work with children like her."

Merrill never came back to school. She was gone during the week, and her aunt came on weekends to help care for her. I still saw her father and brothers in the mornings and late afternoons, but I stayed out of their house and fields. Without Merrill, Kevin and I did not play in the road.

Spring and daylight savings returned. I started after-school gymnastics and French lessons, and didn't get home from school until supper. My parents decided I was old enough to do the dishes, and I did them, standing in front of the steam-fogged window, ignoring the darkness as it fell outside and gradually erased the edges of the McDonoughs' house, graying its yellow until the only definition left was the slice of light at the base of a curtained window. I watched the light and thought of Merrill, how she was unaware of the grace that hung over her like her father's hand, hovering before landing on her tangled hair. And I envied her, for all she was safe from.

The Splendor of Orchids

FROM THE BEGINNING, KENNETH HAD BEEN HONEST ABOUT the fact he was married. He'd told Claire that his marriage was a loveless sham, a convenience, said divorce was imminent now that he had found someone he really cared for; his wife and he had grown apart after marrying too quickly, too young. He came to the city all the time on business; his wife was always out selling Westchester County real estate. They hardly ever saw each other.

He'd gone to Puerto Rico on business, he told Claire—conferences, tedious banquet dinners, golf. And although he wasn't gone for long, one Wednesday night without him (he always "worked late" midweek) helped her to make up her mind: she was tired of waiting. She would tell him she couldn't see him anymore.

She didn't like to think about what had made the others leave, but now—in the confident flush of her decision about Kenneth—she could look coolly at the events of the past.

She'd sent Martin roses and made Gary a dinner that cost more than a hundred dollars at Balducci's (she had taken special pride in ordering fiddlehead ferns out of season, meeting the eyes of the gruff produce manager and cocking her head to say, "Yes, please, no matter what they cost," imagining he knew it was all for a man). Martin had waited two days to call to thank her, and then never called again. Gary stopped sleeping over, saying it wasn't worth it since he got up so early to go running. At least this time, she'd be the one to end things.

So when Kenneth called at the studio the next Monday as she was gathering her things together to ask if she would meet him at the Rainbow Room for a drink, she said No. It was almost eight o'clock, and she was hungry. She was going home, to order in Chinese and put on her sweats. It was supposed to drop to 10 below by midnight. Fine, he'd meet her there, bring a bottle of wine. She had cramps, wanted to go to bed early. It was the strongest she'd ever resisted, and she was sure the cramps would deter him, but he persisted. He'd missed her, he said, wanted to see her; a quiet evening sounded great, he'd show her his photos from Puerto Rico.

It *was* nice to see him, when he walked in the apartment door and his bulky shape filled its frame before he shut it and strode across the wooden floor, scrunching up the rag rug, to kiss her. Her apartment always seemed changed with him in it, as if it couldn't quite contain him. It was more than just his height, although at six feet he was eight inches taller than she; it was something in his energy that made the room seem too small. His voice boomed off the walls, his footsteps pounded, even the sound of his showering seemed too much for the small studio apartment to contain. When he sat on her futon sofa, where she curled up alone so perfectly it was as if it had been custom made, his knees jutted up and his feet slid restlessly under her coffee table, kicking the fallen TV section of the *Times*, stepping on the paperback that had slipped from her hand when he walked in.

"How's your time?"

"I should catch the ten-oh-seven."

Claire looked at the clock radio on the table next to the phone. 8:35. She'd give them until nine.

"How are you feeling?" He was slipping a paper bag from a dark bottle of wine.

She grimaced, held her stomach.

"Aw." He made a sympathetic pout, bent his face with its mane of wifty brown hair toward her.

The buzzer sounded. Claire leapt up, jogged to the intercom, pushed the button. She opened the apartment door, called "Up here," listened to the delivery man climb three flights of stairs with her fragrant moo-shu pork, her favorite hot and sour soup, her little stapled packets of waxed paper holding mustard and soy sauce. He wore a yellow rain slicker although it wasn't raining. Cold lifted off of him in waves. She took the bag and handed him ten dollars. Kenneth had already eaten.

She never got to finish the food, though, because when Kenneth got up to use the bathroom, pounding again across her floor and pushing further askew the slippery rug, she reached in his briefcase for the photos he said were in the pocket, and pulled out a crumpled sheet of paper: a typed itinerary for Mr. and Mrs. Kenneth Cook and Children. At first she thought it was a name, as if another couple, the Childs, had traveled with them. At the two hotels listed, a Master suite was booked, with an additional room having twin beds and a supplemental cot. Three kids. The loud flush of the toilet startled her, the way it always did when someone else used it, and she tucked the itinerary back in the briefcase.

The photos showed palm trees, a rain forest, sugar plantations, pink and green and yellow stucco houses with lacy wrought-iron balconies—none of people except for one of Kenneth standing smiling in a straw hat against a golf cart. Which one of his children had taken that, she wondered. She asked so many questions—what he did, where he ate, whom he met—that she marveled at how smoothly he lied, the ease with which he must have been making things up. The more he talked, the more she froze into not confronting him with what she'd found. She would rely on what she'd planned to say, as if she'd never seen the word *Children*, the words *Supplemental Cot.*

So when he slipped the photos in his inside coat pocket and leaned back, smiling, to stretch his arm toward her, to run his fingers up and down her back, she started. "I can't do this anymore," she said. "You need to work out your own life, your own problems. It's not fair to me, to you, to her."

He didn't put up much of an argument, not as much as she'd hoped. His hand dropped from her back and he looked down at the floor, nodding, his chin almost touching the knot of his tie. He didn't seem to notice how wooden Claire's words sounded, how rehearsed, how obviously echoing with all they weren't saying.

At last he looked up. "I'm sorry. I've asked too much of you. Your patience. Your good will." He reached over and ran his index finger along the curve of her cheek, her jaw bone, and when he reached her throat, she twisted away and stood up.

"I don't want to lose you, Claire."

"You can't have it both ways, you know. If you make a decision, let me know."

"You're right," he said. And then, after standing and shrugging into his camel's hair coat and wrapping his scarf around his neck, "You'll be fine." He bent to kiss the top of her head and walked out the door. She leaned into it when it closed. She had stopped shaking by the time she remembered her half-rolled pancake, her cold soup. Although he'd left, the room was still too small.

She grabbed her coat and hat and gloves, and ran down the stairs to the street. The wind off the river raised dead leaves and bits of trash, whirling them around her feet. Her street ran through an unnumbered wedge of Greenwich Village, between the solid flanks of Seventh Avenue and Hudson Street, a pocket of treelined cobbled streets, old brownstones with blackpainted iron banisters and flower boxes, red townhouses with arches of shadow where the newer brick met the old when stoops had been torn down and original front doors bricked over to turn houses into flats. Nothing was higher than five stories.

She turned north on West Fourth, passing restaurants and florists and cafés, windows steamed with heat and breath, toward the blinking pink neon of the crisply lettered LIQUORS sign, the golden dot of a traffic signal up ahead at Jane Street, the word DELICATESSEN dropping in lit red letters from the cornice of a building, all foreshortened in the black night. It looked like an album cover, a movie still, a poster picture of All Night New York. It would be her lover now, this city with its richness of pleasures in neon, its swirling trash, its aching, vibrant life. It would never lie to her.

The next morning she woke to shovels scraping pathways beneath her window. Curbs disappeared under the snow, parked cars made hunched hills, and off every surface glittered a million reflections of the harsh morning sun. At street intersections, snow had been pushed and mounded into piles taller than most pedestrians, piles that would harden and turn black and melt last of all. Sand and salt and kitty litter dusted the busier sidewalks; footprints became dark pockets of slush. The snow was melting in the sun, but when the temperature dropped again into the single digits at night, it would freeze into sheets of ice.

WHEN THE FIRST HANG-UP CALL CAME, CLAIRE SHRUGGED IT off as random error. But when it happened three times in one night, and the caller didn't hang up but stayed on the line, breathing as Claire heard her own repeated query—"Yes? Hello, yes?"—echo in the apartment, she pulled out the thin silver cord and left the phone disconnected until the next day.

They started coming two, three times a week, either in the late afternoon, four or five, or around ten or eleven at night. Never on weekends. The phone would ring, she'd pick it up, and there'd be a brief moment of imagining Kenneth punching in her number—to say he'd made a mistake, before his wife walked in, and he had to hang up—and then she'd hear the sound of the blizzards engulfing the city, buzzing with the absence of all they blotted out. No, it wasn't Kenneth at the other end of the line, but a shapeless phantom with a pale delicate hand, moonglow fingernails bitten short, blue subdermal veins, holding a receiver, not hanging up.

At work, callers identified themselves. She arrived by eight to find Gerald and Nina hovering over the huge 4 x 5 camera in the middle of the studio, holding light meters and flicking flashes like a wink of sunlight. Harmon's studio was in a loft on the sixth floor of an old warehouse on West Eighteenth Street, two of its walls taken up with huge, single-paned windows that looked out on the leaden sky, the gray and brown buildings of Chelsea blanketed with snow that melted in patches to show tar paper and froze again to shine like glass. Below the windows, steam heaters hissed and banged, but the loft stayed so cold everyone wore mittens and scarves. A kitchen and offices had been built along the inside wall, but Claire worked at one of the long tables set up behind the elevator shaft, where the plants were lined up on counters, tagged and trimmed and misted with atomizers, ready for sacrifice under the hot lamps and the camera's lens. She worked free-lance, eight hours a day to write copy, read galleys and mechanicals, think about flowers, their colors and growing characteristics. This month had been orchids. Next month: poppies.

THE PHONE BECAME THE FIRST THING CLAIRE LOOKED AT IN the morning when she awoke, and the last thing before falling asleep. She turned to it as soon as she walked in the door at the end of the day and watched it all evening as if her stare would keep it from ringing. She started talking to herself whenever she passed in front of the window, drawing the blinds as soon as she got home, and practicing a deep, gruff voice. She learned that if she uncoupled the phone from the machine she didn't have to hear the ring. She didn't even have to say hello.

When she'd gone five days without a hang-up, she thought it was over and was on her way to reconnect the machine to the phone when she stopped, halfway across the room, at the sound of a loud click. The machine beeped twice, flashed its red light and then glowed its green as it played the recorded message she'd changed to eliminate her name and emphasize that "we're not here to take your call." She tiptoed to it, slid up the volume button, and—when all she heard was the moist smack of tongue against palate— pulled the machine's cord firmly from the wall. She went back to doing the dishes, but kept looking over her shoulder, armpits clammy, as though a stranger had entered her apartment and occupied her favorite chair.

IT HAD BEEN IN THE SINGLE DIGITS FOR THREE DAYS IN A ROW. Thin tears of ice ran along the edges of the studio windows, and the plants were blanketed under heavy plastic tarp. The mechanicals were supposed to go to the printer in two days, but Gerald told her not to bother coming in the next day, it was too cold. He photocopied the mechanicals for her, and told her to phone in any mistakes she found.

It was almost eight by the time she reached her apartment door to turn the police lock, drop the deadbolt, and push in. Her purse fell heavily from her shoulder, tugging against her wrist and banging into the grocery bag whose corded handles cut into her bare hand. Slippery magazines and bills slid to the floor. She dropped everything in disgust—keys, gloves, purse, bag, mail—and, in the light from the hall coming through the open door behind her, watched the room contract to the round table next to the armchair. There it sat, crouching, a trick in its passive quiet: the phone. Its red light beamed solid. At least six calls.

She shut the door and moved to the futon, her coat still hanging from her shoulders, to collapse and grab a pillow to her chest. Last summer, when she was between jobs, she had painted the walls of the apartment a pale yellow, a color she'd had mixed specially to match a Pantone swatch. Dressed in a T-shirt and old jeans, she'd opened the windows wide to the sounds of kids playing softball in the playground across the street, the salsa beat of the downstairs neighbors' radio, a breeze that felt clean and fresh against her forehead as she painted. She'd taped the edges carefully, and squared off each wall with a roller's width of paint before filling in the expanse with color. It was a lovely color, with a tinge of peachy warmth. She'd kept the baseboards and window and door trim a glossy linen white. The apartment had been hers then, all hers, but it wasn't any longer. It had been invaded by the phantom, its four walls appropriated by the accusation in the silenced phone.

It had been two weeks since they'd broken up, but she still found herself looking for one of Kenneth's stray socks under the sofa, a tie draped over the back of a chair. Other men had left remnants behind, remnants Claire had kept in place for a while—Martin's toothbrush on the edge of her sink, Gary's sweatshirt on the knob of her closet door—as a way to hold onto the presence of these men who'd slept in her bed, propped their feet on the edge of the tub, draped an arm around her hip as she stirred a delicate sauce, so that by the time the toothbrush found its way to the bucket beneath the sink, silver polish caked at the base of its mashed bristles, and the sweatshirt had been washed and cut into squares for dusting, Claire had made of her apartment a shrine to the masculinity that had passed through its doors. But now, looking around the room, she blinked at her furniture, its shadows looming like stains against the dimness, oddly unfamiliar and startlingly empty.

Now it was just Claire and the red light, the only bright thing in the room. She stood stiffly, removing her coat and walking to the closet. She bent to pick up the scattered mail and her purse and placed them neatly on the dresser. In the kitchen, she pulled the chain of the overhead light and the room filled with brightness. There. She pulled groceries from the bag, put them away, leaving the broccoli and red peppers and two eggs in the sink for dinner. Back in the living room, she pulled the shades, kicked off her cold, damp shoes, and found her thick wool socks under the futon. She walked over to the table and pushed the playback button on the machine. The tape rewound almost half its length, and Claire leaned against the chair, waiting. Five sharp beeps signaled a successful rewind, and then it began to play. Silence. Clicks. Muffled breaths. She made herself listen, holding her hands away from the cords. More clicks. What sounded like a stifled giggle. Then a voice, young, female, but trying to sound older and male so that for a strange, disorienting moment Claire wondered if the tape had somehow captured her own gruff answerings: "Yes, hello? This is a call for Ms Bridgeman." A pleasant voice, if somehow altered; almost professional. "We're taking a survey and would like a moment of your time. Have you ever slept with a married man?" Claire reeled, and moved to stop the machine, but the next message had already started and her hand stilled at the sound of the same voice, fiercer this time: "We must know. How many times have you slept with a married man?"

Claire pulled her hands to her stomach, pressing her palms against the narrow barrel of her ribcage. Beneath the soft wool of her sweater, her upper arms were clammy. Who would know? They had to be cranks. Kids looking in the Manhattan phone directory for the giveaway of a single woman: first initial, no address. It was a coincidence. It had to be. But then, just as she felt her body relax with a release of breath, came the whispered reminder, its tone a threat: "Adultery is a sin," and Claire's right hand fluttered out from under her arm to hit the playback button, yank the cord from the jack, put out the red light.

Her window shades were thick, but not opaque, and later that night, when she went to bed, the image of her shadow moving behind them was enough to make her crouch on the floor and crawl to the table, click off the lamp, undress in the dark.

IT WAS NICE AND QUIET WORKING AT HOME; SHE KEPT HER feet in the wool socks and drank mugs of herbal tea. Outside the window, just beyond the reflection of her lamp hovering against the glass, the sky stayed the same gray all day; no wind rattled the bare branches of the ginkgo tree against the fire escape. She felt as though she were inside a cloud.

By four o'clock she'd checked the mechanicals three times, slugging the captions and verifying all botanical names. She found a few minor corrections, things Gerald could fix with a knife, and called the studio. On her hands and knees to plug in the phone and machine, she knew she couldn't leave her phone disconnected forever. She was a freelancer, after all.

Gerald was in the middle of a shoot, would call her right back. So Claire didn't think twice when the phone rang a few minutes later. But when she said, "Hi, you ready?" and there was no response, something sank in her belly. A quick intake of breath and a voice, the same as the night before, distressingly polite: "Claire Bridgeman, please."

"Who's calling?" Her own voice was sharp.

"Claire Bridgeman is a slut. Claire Bridgeman fucks married men." The voice was still so polite that as Claire slammed down the receiver, her heart pounding, she wondered if she was overreacting. She pulled the cord and held it in her hand for ten minutes, then plugged it back in to call Gerald, telling him that she'd had to run out before the deli across the street closed. They went over the corrections, and Gerald reminded her of Harmon's policy that the actual mechanicals had to be signed off on before going to the printer, not just the photocopies. She'd need to come in the next day. He told her, "Hey, stay warm tonight. Stay *in*," and when her hand peeled off the receiver, it left a starfish of moisture on the smooth white plastic.

Now she knew the calls weren't from Richard's wife, either, but whenever she started to consider who they were from, she'd stop at the fact that she'd been found out. And fast on the heel of that fact was another, whose sharpness stunned her on the treacherous streets on her bundled way to the studio the next morning, her eyes no farther than the patch of ice her next footstep would avoid: He was married, and she'd known it all along.

THEY CLOSED THE EXOTICS CATALOG, AND AT THE END OF THE day, Gerald handed her an orchid to take home. At first, she resisted. An orchid required a great deal of care, she knew; she'd written the copy detailing frequent misting and proper drainage in porous rock or chips of bark. But then he said, "The splendor of Phalanopsis brings sophistication and understated elegance to any living space," quoting her own words, which he'd set in four different display fonts before finalizing the layout. So she smiled and took it.

She wrapped it—it *was* a Phalanopsis, lavender and magenta with faint etchings of red—in layers, first a paper tent over its delicate pillow of a bud, then plastic sheeting loosely over that, followed by a blanket of bubble wrap, and lastly, placed it in the cardboard box she found under the sink and sprinkled Styrofoam worms all around it.

But in the narrow vestibule downstairs, her carefully arranged bundles failed her. With full hands Claire had no way of opening the door. She propped her knee against the wall and balanced the box on her thigh, pulled on her hat, tightened her scarf around her neck, lifted her purse strap over her head, fingered in her pocket for a subway token, and opened the heavy door, sticking a booted foot in the space to hold it open. Cold rushed in, tossing snow onto the wet floor. She gathered her bundles to her chest and pushed out. It had been snowing since noon. In the failing four o'clock light the freshly fallen drifts looked blue.

The subway was only half a block away, but snow gathered quickly in the creases of her coat sleeves. She reached the station steps, mounded with layers of ice, clouded white and jet black, frosted on top with fresh snow, and descended carefully. Even in the cold, the corridor reeked of urine and disinfectant, and looking ahead through the bulb-lit gloom, she stopped. In less than twenty minutes, she'd be turning the key in the door of her apartment and walking in to where the phone machine waited, messages lurking in its silver tape.

She ran back up to the street, to air that didn't stink but tingled her nose and throat, toward the lights draped on the bare branches of the trees along Seventh Avenue, and into the back seat of a taxi that had just let someone out at the corner. She told the driver the Met and he slapped down the metal flag. It was an older cab, without a thick plastic wall between front seat and back, and Claire leaned forward into the open space.

"Take Sixth Avenue, please."

The cab braked through the slush to turn east on Sixteenth Street. "Hell of a night to be going anywhere."

She leaned back against the sloping seat. "Mm."

"We're in for another big one."

"Oh?"

In the rear view mirror, his eyes were brilliant blue under bushy brows. The pale skin on the back of his neck looked soft above a wool scarf and below bristles of short, dark hair. "Yep. Some system's moving down from Canada, gonna hit early morning. No one's going nowhere tomorrow. Ain't seen anything like it in forty, fifty years, they say."

"It's been snowing all afternoon." Claire tilted her head and licked her lips. Chapped. His eyes met hers in the mirror. She turned her head, sat up straight.

"This is nothing." His hand moved to his hair, smoothed it. "City's gonna shut down. Hope you live close to the Met."

"No, I live downtown." Claire crossed her legs.

He laughed. "Well, then I hope you got the shoes."

She smiled, looked out the window. "I have an orchid in my care," she announced. "A rare, valuable flower."

"A florist, huh?"

"No. I'm a copywriter for a garden catalog."

"What catalog? I get a lot."

"Harmon's Garden Catalog."

"Don't know it." Their eyes met again in the mirror. "Not Victoria's Secret?"

Claire felt a smile, prim, and looked away. "Not exactly."

Outside the window, the stilled, white city passed, hulking cast-iron buildings of Sixth Avenue giving way, after the dullness of shut-up second floor envelope-and-box printers, streetfront florists, sweatshop garment factories, the blackened brick and limestone of the upper Twenties and Thirties, to the billboard jazz of Times Square where high up on a dark building in LED letters the national debt spun frantically to the fourth decimal point, to the hard-edged, moneyed glass-and-steel glitter of midtown. Then the city fell, suddenly at Fifty-ninth Street opposite the grand hotels, into the dark park where black branches bent with fallen snow and lamplight glowed against stone bridges and shone on frozen ponds. Something fell in Claire, too, to anonymity and quiet, and when she looked up toward the front seat again, the cabbie was shaking his big head, shaggy hair swaying above a thick neck, and softly repeating, "The Met." She felt the bones in her own hands moving, and looked into her lap to see her fists clenching and unclenching. Kenneth was wrong. She wasn't fine at all.

The cab stopped in front of the museum. Snow fell in big, wet clumps, and she walked toward the huge banners above the front steps, which proclaimed DEGAS, ALEXANDRIAN SCULPTURE, JAPANESE WOODCUTS in white letters on fabric whose color looked leeched by the gray dusk. In the entryway, overhead space heaters spilled hot air. A blue-uniformed guard raised a hand. "Check your packages, please."

Straight ahead, a profusion of lilies and tulips and long, serpentine branches of pussy willow exploded from a huge porcelain vase atop a marble pedestal. Piano music tinkled down from the mezzanine. People—not a crowd but enough to fill the lobby with a buzz of voices—milled about in small clusters, consulting guidebooks and museum floor plans. Only visitors from out of town would come here on a night like this.

Claire felt her spirits lift: the allure of anonymity still tugged at her, but now she felt vital, pulsing, a native among tourists. Holding her head high, she walked to the checkroom, where she checked her wraps and box, and then down the hall, past the roped-off floor mosaic of Medusa and the Greek statues, to the ladies' room. With every step, she felt the drama she carried grow more noticeable, a cloak of mystery trailing her, a wake of speculation. Surely these people could sense that she lived a life of strange phone calls, of thwarted attraction, of a lover cheating on his wife for her.

But when she pushed through the swinging door and walked toward her reflection in the mirror above the row of sinks, she stopped. There was no mystery—only her hairline dotted with light freckles and swirled with hat-flattened auburn curls, her lips loose and dry with squares of chapped skin, her high, curved forehead beaded with perspiration. Saliva pooled at her back teeth and she tasted tin foil. She leaned against a basin and turned on the taps. She yanked her hands away: the water was scalding. Moving quickly to a stall, she bent over the toilet, but nothing happened. She turned around, lifted and pulled down her clothing, sat. Nothing. Back at the sink, she splashed her face with cold water and forced herself to meet her own eyes, whispering "Okay, okay," a metronome beat. Her hands, almost green in the fluorescent light, looked small and forlorn under the heavy fall of water.

She pressed a paper towel to her face until she felt moisture seep through and worked a comb through her tangled hair. She held her own wrists, briefly, her thumbs and middle fingers making twin bracelets. Then she pushed out the door and hurried down the hall, through the lobby and up the stairs, past somber canvases of dour-faced nobility and dark resurrections, and into the nineteenth-century European

collection: feverishly pink cheeks of Renoir maidens, Van
Gogh's insistently peaked waves of paint. Against a wall,
Rodin's Adam and Eve hunched in sorrow and shame, and just
past them, she turned a corner to Degas' bronze castings.

A ballerina stood under a glass dome, on her own pedestal,
in a stiff, faded net tutu. Her head was lifted like a bud on the
stem of her neck, one foot forward so her weight slung in the
balance of jutting hips, a real blue satin ribbon tied neatly
around a bronze plait of hair. Alone in the gallery, Claire
placed her feet in what she remembered as fourth position, her
own belly heavy and dull. It was there she'd felt desire, sharp
and quick, when she first knew she'd take Kenneth into her
bed, as they sat in a dark corner of an Italian restaurant, feet
touching under the table, her small fingers in his large hands.
The ballerina's eyes were closed and her head was back, her
face pure and serene, free from the complications of desire.

The painting Claire had come to see, without knowing it
until she found herself in front of it, was *Pygmalion and
Galatea.* Galatea's feet and calves, as fish-white as the block of
marble they rose from, climbed to flushed thighs and buttocks
and a dimpled back, shiny brown hair, arms that protested
Pygmalion's too ardent admiration of what he's wrought. He's
dropped his chisel and pushed a furtive hand on Galatea's
breast. In the background of the painting, on a shelf beneath a
puddly cupid, two masks open their mouths in a scream.

The crisp squeak of rubber on marble announced a guard
in blue uniform. "Museum's closing in fifteen minutes."

SNOW WAS STILL FALLING, LESS CLUMPY NOW BUT FASTER, AND
sticking. As she moved to the top of the steps, it whirred and
spun around her face, around the blinking red DON'T WALK
sign at the curb, around the fountain, drained for winter, at
the bottom of the steps, around the rectangles of warm yellow

light made by the windows across Fifth Avenue. Claire took small steps, as if to lighten her weight, and held the polished brass railing with a gloved hand.

She walked. The man in the coat check, whose mustached, sallow face reminded her of Lech Walesa's, had found an abandoned Bloomingdale's shopping tote for her, so the orchid was easier to carry. The snow was falling light and dry now, and there was no wind. On the sidewalk, her feet shuffled their way through drifts of fresh powder. She passed a few people, dog walkers and the occasional bundled pedestrian heading resolutely home, chins tucked into fine wool overcoats or shaggy furs. Six o'clock felt like midnight. Haloes of illuminated snow surrounded the globular street lamps and, twenty-five blocks away, the tall buildings of midtown disappeared in a smudgy yellow glow. The city was quiet, muted, yet under her feet and in her fingertips it hummed and pulsed, alive.

At 79th Street, a bus would lumber alongside her and she would climb aboard, drop the token from earlier into the coinbox, slump into a window seat. Her fingers and toes would tingle and her face would slacken in the warmth. Drowse would overwhelm her, seeping into her bones like ink into paper, and she'd feel her lids grow heavy, her mouth dry. At home, she would lift the box from the Bloomingdale's tote and place it on the table. She would pull a blanket around her and burrow into the futon and dream of snow surrounding her, falling dry and soft over the bump of her shoulder, the curve of her hip, the slope where her stomach dipped, and accumulating in the creases and bends of her clothes and body to make of her a generally round mound. With the falling snow would come whirring white noise ending in a hush as big as a roar, one big pillow of oblivion.

The snow would not be cold; it was only the air that was cold, she thought as she lifted her face into it, and when she threw open the windows, that air would chase from her apartment Kenneth's shadow and shape, the phone's incipient ring, the sting of her guilt. And she would sleep. When she awoke, she would sit up to a thick finger of snow on the narrow ledge outside her window, a painfully bright blue sky, and she would shake from her hair and the coat still around her body the flakes of fallen snow. She would pick up the silver cord and trail her hand along it back to the jack and plug it in. She would call New York Telephone and order a new number, and then she would turn to the window's bright light and see the box on the table. She would unwrap the orchid and find its magenta blossom sprung from its testicular bud. And she would marvel at the hairline netting in its petals, now backlit by sunlight and as intricate as veins.

What Her Sister Wanted

THE KITCHEN SMELLED OF BURNED BUTTER. JAMIE WAS interested less in intentions than in results, so the fact that her mother was baking Tammi's birthday cake from scratch did not make up for the fact that something went wrong whenever she baked. Her mother was always rushed, and steps got out of order. She'd start paying bills while waiting for milk to heat, phoning while water boiled, or doing the dishes while butter melted, and then forget. Milk scalded, water boiled over, butter burned.

Jamie walked into the apartment batting the air in front of her as if the smoke were made up of tiny gnats. Her mother was on the phone. Jamie dropped her knapsack on the dining table and walked to the stove, turned off the flame. Her mother's head was bent over a pile of bills and coupon flyers, but she looked up, smiled. "Thanks, baby." She lowered her chin to the phone again. "Yeah, I'm here. Galvin. G-A-L... How much? Okay. I'll try to get it in the mail next week. All right. Thanks."

Jamie busied herself with the plastic bowls and metal beater blades and rubber spatulas and a big wooden spoon, carrying them to the sink where she squirted them with a green worm of detergent and opened the faucet. Galvin was their last name—hers, her mother's, Tammi's, and although he didn't live with them anymore, Daddy's.

"The cake's in the oven, baby. But I botched the frosting."

"I'll make more."

"No, you sit down. I need to think, I need to clean this up—" and she steered Jamie out of the small kitchen, its counters covered with cereal boxes and twisty-ties and breakfast dishes, opened sticky jars of jam and peanut butter, a heel of bread. "I'll bring you a soda. Start your homework."

Jamie sat down at the dining table, pushing aside her mother's purse and sweater and her sister's coloring books. She hated these chairs, the way they wobbled, the way her skin stuck moistly to their plastic seats, the way the chair legs cut circles into the linoleum floor. But most of all she hated the way the fourth chair was used now, pushed against the wall as a surface for the overflow from the table's clutter. Daddy used to sit in that chair, talking loudly and tapping her mother's wrist with his fingers when he made a joke. Sometimes he'd get strict with Jamie, tell her to finish eating and stop interrupting, and once when Tammi blew bubbles in her milk, he slammed his fist down so hard Tammi spilled the cup and Jamie, who had been chewing, bit her tongue. But usually he drank from a beer can next to his plate and laughed, showing Jamie once how to run her fingers so fast through the flame from his lighter that she wouldn't feel the heat. Her mother must have noticed the difference, too, because she never laughed the way she used to when all four chairs were used, when the one for Tammi had held a red booster seat she'd since outgrown.

Jamie's next spelling bee was in a week, against Ms Marshall's fourth graders, and while a week seemed as distant to her as her driver's license, Jamie was a child who curled up to preparation as a comfort. Mr. Anderson had just given her a new speller, and she bent her head to inhale its fresh plasticky aroma and opened it, smoothing the pages on either side. She sharpened her pencil into the book's gutter, then tapped the shavings into her palm, carried them to the sink. She dusted her hands, rinsed and dried them. Her mother stood holding the refrigerator door open with her hip while she put away the milk and orange juice, passed Jamie a fruit soda. Jamie opened it and carried it back to her speller, took a gulp. She blew away the remaining graphite dust, picked up her pencil. When she met the first word, she was giddy from holding herself back. She considered "ei" and "ie," how they were sometimes easy, like "science" or "friend" but other times much trickier, like with a silent "g." These words thrilled her. Sounding them out didn't work. The only way to know them was to memorize them. And she was an ace at memorization. She had nothing to worry about from fourth graders.

"Hey, sillybones." Her mother's nicknames for her and Tammi changed every few months. As a toddler, Jamie had been Sandcrab because of the way she crawled, lowering her forehead to the carpet and pushing like a plow. Then, in first grade, she'd been Jamelia, a name her mother made up as response to both Jamie's complaint one day that she had a boy's name and her favorite book, *Amelia Bedelia*. She'd recently become Sillybones—or sometimes Bookworm—not because she was especially silly but because her mother said she wished she were. Tammi was Ninja Girl, although as Jamie could have told her mother, her little sister's affections had moved on to killer whales, especially the huge glossy one on the Marine World commercial.

Her mother was bent over the oven. "Come help me frost Tammi's cake. You can lick the spoon."

Jamie put down her pencil and went into the kitchen. Her mother placed the cake on the counter. It was a chocolate bundt that drooped on one side. Her mother pulled a clean knife from the drying rack. "Here," she said, placing the bowl of fresh icing on the counter.

Jamie touched the warm cake. It smelled delicious. "I think you're supposed to let it cool first."

"I suppose you are. Okay, we'll let it cool." Her mother scooped a glob of white icing into her mouth. "Have some while we wait." She held out the knife to Jamie, who bent over the bowl and ran the knife blade around the sides to scrape off the thin dried drips.

Jamie knew about patience from Daddy. She remembered sitting on his lap while he held a big book in front of her. His voice, low and quiet, paused frequently so her eyes could take in the colorful pictures. Even then, Jamie had been drawn to the scratchy black marks at the bottom of the page, and it wasn't until her father's arms jerked a bit around her, to lift the book from where it was slipping against her knees, and he said, "Hey, check out the lion under the tree" or "There's little Madeline, last in line," that Jamie looked away from the lines of type. He always gave her time, sipping from the bottle on the arm of the big stuffed chair they sat in, his arm around her back so she couldn't knock the bottle over. Sometimes he fell asleep, dropping the book completely, and sweet stale breath would escape from his open mouth. Her mother would come in the room then, lift Jamie off his lap and carry her away to bed. And then, usually, Jamie would lie in bed listening to her parents' shouts. Once she got out of bed and found her mother standing in front of that same chair, her bathrobe sleeve off her shoulder and her mouth open as if to cry. But when she saw Jamie, she clapped her hand over her mouth and collapsed, whatever making her fall hidden by the back of the chair. Some of the words her parents used Jamie had heard before on the playground, seen carved in bathroom doors. Others she hadn't. Jamie didn't mind when Daddy fell asleep reading to her. She'd curl further into his chest and wonder why some letters were short and round, others tall and thin.

Her mother lifted another gob of icing to her mouth, leaned back against the counter, lit a cigarette.

"You said you were quitting."

"I was." Her mother rolled her eyes, lifted the pack out of a drawer. "When these are gone, no more." She shrugged, turned to the sink, rinsed out a cup, turned off the tap. "Nicotine is addictive, Jamie, stronger than any resolution."

Jamie sounded out the syllables to herself, *re-so-lu-tion*, and then, when she knew she had it, said, "Mr. Anderson says smoking makes your lungs black as coal."

Her mother inhaled again, then blew smoke out. "I know." She tamped the cigarette against the wet end of the faucet, dropped it in the sink. Her eyes shone, the irises of her brown eyes seeming to merge with the pupils to make big dark dots. "Don't grow up so fast on me, okay, baby? Sometimes I think I don't know you any more."

For two months now, Jamie had been getting up before her mother to make her own lunches on school days. She liked walking to the store on her own, adding two columns of figures, tucking herself in bed. Sometimes she'd fake sleep and wait until the light under her mother's bedroom door went out, to go lie in the big chair, where she'd wake up disoriented to find the living room light on and a corner of her old baby blanket bunched in her fist. She hadn't had a temper tantrum in months.

Her mother glanced at her watch, pushed away from the counter, grabbed her purse from the chair. "Time to go get Tammi. Hide the cake in the cupboard, would you? I'll frost it in the morning before she gets up. We'll need five candles, remember. One to grow on." She opened the screen door, rubbed the toe of her shoe on the dirty patch of carpet that got wet whenever it rained, shook her head. "The balloons are in with the silverware. You can hide them in my closet if you want to blow them up."

"Okay."

The screen door banged shut. But Jamie wanted to finish the chapter first. *Eight. Ate. Rain. Rein. Reign.* These would take some time.

DADDY HAD BEEN GONE FOR NINE MONTHS. "JUST US GIRLS now," their mother had told them the first night without him, all three of them lying on her unmade bed. The sheets had pulled back into a twisted heap at her mother's feet, and Jamie had stared at the patches of bare toenail where the polish had smudged off. "We'll take care of each other just fine," her mother had said, and pressed each daughter to her warm, soft body.

At first, Jamie heard her mother talking about him on the phone a lot, changing her voice when Jamie walked into the room. But when Jamie asked if she could visit him, her mother said that wasn't such a good idea. When she asked her mother why they all weren't still together, her mother said Daddy needed to get better and Jamie would understand when she was older.

Her mother's lips got thinner, her eyes more worried. Daddy became a secret and a forbidden word. One night Jamie explained that she wouldn't eat carrots because Daddy didn't like them, either. "That's nothing to be proud of," her mother had said. "Those carrots cost money, and not his." Jamie took to writing "Walter" on the back of her spelling book and speaking the name silently to herself before closing her mouth to keep it inside. She would hear it in her mother's voice sometimes, when she was working on her speller or crossing the playground to the bus, and then it sounded as sudden and urgent as a gull's cry or a fog horn traveling across the bay. She would look up then, and try to place it in her memory, but she couldn't, and when she tried capturing it again, sounding out the syllables in her own voice, the word was as muffled and faint as if she had spoken it through a pillow.

Usually at dinner Jamie pretended to herself that Daddy had just gone down the hall to wash his hands and would be right back to pull the fourth chair to the table, sit, and waggle his eyebrows at her and Tammi. Or maybe, like her friend Jeannette's dad, he was working late and would be home after she and Tammi went to bed. Jamie liked to imagine what kind of job he would have, and couldn't decide between a plumber and an electrician. His hands, she remembered, were caked with dirt under the nails and he would stand at the sink for minutes sudsing with detergent while around him rose clouds of steam. So when Tammi announced that night that she'd seen Daddy and invited him to her birthday party, Jamie almost didn't breathe.

Her mother kept pouring milk into Tammi's glass as she stared at her youngest daughter. The milk spilled onto the plastic placemat, bright with a design of zoo animals. "Shit!" Her mother slammed the carton down in the puddle of milk and asked, quieter, "Where?"

"I saw Daddy buying things, like us." Out of Tammi's mouth, the word carried no risk of retort.

"Buying what things? Where?" Her mother sat now, peering at Tammi.

"Mrs. Coffey let me get Life Savers. Julie took the yellow one, but I saved the red for later. I'll go get it." Tammi started pushing back her chair, but her mother stopped it with her hand.

"Where, Tammi? Where did you see him?"

"I want the red Life Saver. I'll show you it."

"Later, for dessert. Answer my question." Her mother's hand moved from the back of Tammi's chair to the table as she leaned forward, her two elbows just missing the pool of spilled milk, and lifted her clasped hands to her mouth, chewed her thumbnails. "Sweetie," she added, and then, "Did Mrs. Coffey take you shopping with her?"

Tammi nodded.

"At Lucky's?"

Tammi shook her whole head from side to side.

"At Safeway?"

Another shake.

"Where?"

"Across from the cars."

Her mother frowned, questions worrying her forehead.

"The cars go really fast."

"What store, Tammi?"

"I think she means the 7-Eleven, Mom, over by the freeway." Her mother looked desperately at Jamie, and Jamie felt suddenly afraid. But then Tammi made an exaggerated nod, one big swipe up and down, her face almost landing in her sliced hot-dog, and picked up a piece with her teeth, and her mother was a mother again, lifting Tammi's chin and pointing to her fork: "You know better than that."

Jamie had been to the 7-Eleven after school for Slurpies and candy and change for the gumball machines. A group of men always stood outside by the phone booth, where the receiver hung loose from its metal cord; the one time Jamie had lifted it to her ear (the men had been fewer that day, and sitting on the curb in the sunshine), it had given no dial tone even after she put in a dime. The men never said anything to Jamie, but she always walked quickly past them, staring at the bird-stained curb, their worn shoes and scruffy pants cuffs vaguely familiar. *Unreliable* was a word her mother often used about her father. It was a good word. She had beaten Billy Ramos with it the week before.

JAMIE KNEW HER SISTER WANTED TO GO TO MARINE WORLD, and it wasn't just the way Tammi talked about killer whales. It was the way she watched the commercial, which came on more frequently now that the park had opened up only ten miles away. She'd stop playing to listen to the upbeat music, her sweet young face uplifted to watch the happy blond family walk hand in hand through the admissions gate, the sleek wet killer whale splashing the crowd, the pretty woman standing on the shoulders of the handsome man on water skis, the park's logo rising on a screen humming with static. Tammi had a dreamy way about her that seemed to ask and expect nothing, so that she almost faded into the background. It wasn't that she was plain or dull or easy to look past. Not at all. With her fine blond curls and round, smoothly lidded brown eyes and quick, open smile, Tammi attracted attraction from strangers in a way Jamie never had. Nor was Tammi quiet. But she voiced no demands, and that made Jamie ache for her, because her sister's longing was all the more powerful for being unspoken.

So Tammi watched TV and played with her blocks, while Jamie did her spelling and their mother washed the dishes, swept the floor, ruffled through the stack of bills. And though each of them was focused on a separate task, seemingly unaware of what the other two were doing, they were all three as connected as one of those giant fungi that Mr. Anderson had told Jamie's class that day were the largest living organisms (not the blue whale, as Allegra Gomez had suggested—a pretty good guess, Jamie had to admit). Clusters of mushrooms would sprout up miles apart, Mr. Anderson had said, seemingly independent and isolated but in truth only a very small, visible part of something vast and hidden, spreading underground like oil, as huge as a whole forest.

Daddy had been back once, less than a week after he moved out. It had been a Thursday, her mother's day off, so she usually picked up Jamie at the curb in the car, or if the weather was nice, came by foot to walk her home. It was the only time Jamie had her mother to herself, but since Daddy had left, her mother had less to say, although she talked more. Going on and on about the houses they walked past, what color paint she liked on which house, or who'd done a nice job of planting their front yard. It seemed pointless to Jamie, since they'd never had a garden of their own and her mother couldn't even keep the jade plant on the deck outside their apartment alive.

In first grade Jamie had been embarrassed by her mother showing up on foot, but now the noisy used station wagon with its sickly idle was even worse. But on this Thursday, her mother hadn't shown up at all, and Jamie sat on the railing, toes curled under the pipe, and wondered if she had decided to cast away the whole family, one at a time, like outgrown articles of clothing. A teacher asked Jamie if she needed a ride, and Jamie shook her head, and after another half hour of waiting, worrying about men that might show up and offer her candy, began the walk home. When she got there, the apartment door was ajar and one of the voices took her a minute to place, as if Mister Rogers had come by to visit.

Her parents fell silent as she walked in, and after she ran to Daddy and breathed in his smell, the room stayed too quiet. Her mother stood near the table, arms crossed against her chest, face pale. "Jamie, sweetie, go into your room," she said, and her father had nodded. "Listen to your mom." And then her mother smiled very kindly at her, so she felt strong enough to ask, "Daddy? Will you be here when I come out of my room?"

He'd only shaken his head, not even looking at her, and her mother had repeated, "Jamie, please. In your room. Daddy'll say good-bye before he goes."

But he didn't. Jamie didn't remember how long she'd waited in her room, but she did remember that when she finally came out, her mother was standing at the sink peeling potatoes so that when Jamie said, "Where is he? You promised!" and her mother replied, "He had to leave" without turning around, the blame fell on both her mother and the curls of potato skin that fell to the floor, flecks flying so fast from the peeler that Jamie winced.

THE PHONE RANG AS TAMMI WAS GETTING INTO HER PAJAMAS and Jamie putting away her books. Their mother had moved to the table to write checks, and pushed back her chair. Usually the chair legs squeaked against the linoleum floor when someone got up from the table, but tonight her mother stood so slowly they didn't make a sound.

"Hello? All right, I'll accept." She paused, her head bent toward the wall, and then said, "Hold on," placed the receiver on the counter, stared at it for a moment, and walked down the hall. Her bedroom door opened, and Jamie heard her speak in a low voice. Then she returned to hang up the phone. "It's my boss, girls, about overtime. I need privacy. You just keep getting ready for bed." Although her mother smiled, her eyebrows pinched together above her nose. She walked back down the hall, and when she closed the bedroom door, Jamie stood up and lifted the receiver slowly, easing her finger off the hang-up button until she heard her mother's voice. "Amazed," it was saying. "I'm amazed you remember her birthday considering where you were when she was born. Kids say a lot of things, Walt. She's only four."

Tammi had both legs in the pajamas, once Jamie's, and had just remembered to check along the elastic for the tag.

"Ten o'clock means ten o'clock," her mother was saying now, and then, "Say all you want, but I'll believe it when I see it."

Jamie hung up gently, sat down next to her sister, pulled the p.j. top over Tammi's head. "Remember that time at the zoo?" she asked. "The gorilla was throwing stuff, remember, his poo and stuff—" Jamie made a face and Tammi laughed.

Daddy had thrown it back, Jamie remembered, and he and the ape had gotten into a tossing battle, making other visitors laugh and a few kids cry. Jamie would have been scared, too, when the gorilla first stood up and glared at them over his shoulder, if Daddy hadn't been there. An Alpha Male, Daddy had explained to her and Tammi on the drive home, after the zookeeper had walked them to the gate. Jamie had wanted to tell her mother, but Daddy said it was better as their secret.

"Gorilla," Tammi repeated, and the two of them pounded their chests, rolling on the floor and laughing so hard Jamie saw nothing on her sister's face but pure glee.

HER MOTHER WORE HER WORN CHENILLE BATHROBE, HER FEET hanging over the arm of the big chair, an ashtray next to her bent knees, watching a late movie. The room was dark except for the TV, its colors glowing against the walls and the chrome ribs of the dining chairs. On the kitchen counter, a bag of potato chips made a dark shadow. Jamie wondered if she could make it there and back without her mother hearing. But her mother turned just then and looked straight at her, lifting her eyebrows: "You having trouble sleeping too?"

Jamie nodded. "I want a glass of milk."

"Okay."

The open refrigerator door cast a lozenge of yellow light on the dark floor, and Jamie stood in it as she reached for a glass from the dishdrainer and filled it halfway with milk. After settling the carton back on its shelf, she reached her hand into the bag of chips, timing the closing of the refrigerator with the rustle of the bag. She scooped two fistfuls into a pouch she made from turning under the elastic waistband of her p.j.s. She carried her glass and began to sidle out of the room.

"Jamie, there's something I need to tell you."

She stopped. The rug itched her bare feet.

"Come here." Her mother reached out with the remote control and muted the TV. Jamie backed into the chair, and sat holding the pouch of chips in a cupped palm. She drank from the glass of milk with the other hand.

Her mother smoothed Jamie's hair down her back, lifted her chin. "You barely ate any dinner. You're going to waste away."

Jamie took another sip of milk.

"You have none of my genes, you know. I put on weight so easily. I guess I should be grateful, but I wish you took after me in something. You're too young to be so thin." Her mother brushed her fingers, acrid with cigarette smoke, against Jamie's cheek. "Look at you. You're the image of your father: your hair, your eyes, your skinniness. The way you watch me." She shook her head, but her fingers were gentle.

"Do I really look a lot like Daddy?" Jamie had kept the word inside for so long, it felt as though she were giving up something to let it out, and she almost wanted her mother to get angry so she could have it back again.

But her mother smiled. "Yeah, you do." She rubbed Jamie's hair between two fingers, then spoke quickly as if changing her mind. "Can you keep a secret?"

Jamie held her hands very still, nodded.

"I got this coupon at Lucky today." Her mother stood up, walked to the counter, where she rummaged through some papers, retrieved a scrap of paper from under the day's mail, waved it. "Discount admission at Marine World if we get there before ten."

"Marine World?"

"She really wants to go, don't you think? It'll be her birthday surprise." Her mother walked back to her, took the now-empty glass from Jamie's hand and, placing it next to the ashtray on the fat arm of the chair, said, "It's late. You better trundle along. Remember, don't say anything to your sister. And brush your teeth again after that milk, okay?"

Jamie did, after she spilled the potato chips into the toilet because she didn't want them anymore and dusted their crumbs off the seat. Back in bed, Jamie fumbled in the top drawer of the bedside table and pulled out the card Daddy had sent her six months before. It played "Happy Birthday" when opened, and she'd opened it so many times the tune had worn out. But she kept it in her drawer, opened it under the covers just in case. "Tammi," she whispered, but her sister's slobbery breathing rose and fell steadily from the bed next to hers. Headlights from the road streaked across the ceiling. Somewhere in the building a door slammed, and then a toilet flushed. Jamie clutched the card, and rolled to face her sister's bed. She wasn't worried about the things she'd heard her mother say on the phone. She knew she understood Daddy better than her mother did. Hadn't he told her so once, murmured in her hair that she was his best girl, his honey for life? Tammi would get what she wanted. She wouldn't be disappointed.

Jamie scrunched into her pillow and thought about the surprise of two *p*s, the single *s*. But when she finally fell asleep, it was not to dream of words but of a wall of bottles, brown and green and amber and clear, empty and full of liquid, stacked tightly on top of one another. No shelves supported them, no paneling or plasterboard stood behind them. The wall was just curved glass, glistening and reflecting light from above, still and balanced until it began to wobble, slowly at first, almost imperceptibly, then in a wave of undulating glass that tumbled down breaking and splashing and with it shrieking and screaming until the shatter and crash became a whimpering cry and a rising howl of a voice, louder and louder until she woke to the image of broken glass on the floor of their kitchen, a memory just behind the curtain of consciousness.

TAMMI STILL SLEPT, FACE FLUSHED, MOUTH WIDE OPEN, ARMS flung over her blankets, when Jamie woke up. In the kitchen, her mother looked up from the coffee she was pouring into a mug, and though her face looked bleary, soft and smudged, Jamie saw in it the source of Tammi's prettiness: blond hair curling back from a widow's peak, dimples, curves. Nothing of herself. Daddy had straight, dark hair; nostrils that broadened over his open-mouthed grin; eye teeth that glinted; the faint shadow of a beard over narrow, chiseled cheeks and chin. Jamie sometimes peered in the mirror but found only her own face, while the memory of his features shifted like tumbling glass chips in a rotated kaleidoscope.

When Tammi came in the kitchen at eight, dragging her blanket across the floor, her mother picked her up and swooped her droopy body into a chair at the table. "My baby," she said, presenting her with a yellow balloon, "my birthday baby," and, to Jamie, "my big girl" and a blue balloon. Her mother kept touching them both, smoothing their hair, patting the tops of their heads, kissing their foreheads. Jamie stayed at the table after she'd finished her cereal, twisting her foot around one of the metal chair legs and watching her mother move around the kitchen, in and out of the bedroom.

She wanted to wear her favorite party dress, and her mother let her, although it no longer fit well and the hem had started to unravel. But her mother found a safety pin, touched up the dress with the iron, and declared it presentable, especially with Jamie's green cardigan over it to hide the straining buttons.

By nine-thirty they were ready to leave, but their mother kept opening cupboards, putting away dishes, wiping the counter, closing drawers. Finally she said, "Okay, let's go," pulling her purse onto her shoulder and patting her sweater pocket for the car keys. She opened her eyes wide and smiled: "Marine World, here we come!"

Tammi ran to the front door, pulling herself up short at the jamb. "Killer whale!" she shouted, running out from beneath her mother's arm, outstretched to hold open the screen door. The light rain that had started during the night had stopped during breakfast, leaving puddles in the apartment parking lot and on the hood of the car. Through her halfway-rolled-down window, Jamie could smell the eucalyptus trees along the freeway, their menthol released by the rain, sharp and fresh over a layer of car exhaust.

They arrived at the main gates just before ten. Their mother didn't even slow down before shepherding Jamie and Tammi through one of the turnstiles, handing the coupon to the man in the cage. Once inside the gates, Jamie paused to pull up her socks and look around at the benches. Her mother wasn't even looking. They had their picture taken at the Porpoise Pool and rode the Safari Shuttle because Tammi liked its yellow fringe and zebra striped awning. At the hamburger stand, their mother went back for extra packets when Tammi asked for more ketchup on her already drenched bun. Their mother touched their heads a lot and gazed off into space. She didn't light a single cigarette. They left the park after going back to the killer whale show a second time, and buying Tammi a small, stuffed replica of Ophelia, the show's two-ton star who splashed the joyously shrieking crowd up to the top row of the bleachers with each flopping fall of her gigantic, glistening body. Tammi was thrilled to find herself soaked, and was still squeezing her shirt dry as they walked toward the gates and the car.

Jamie was walking along, staring at the ground, at different colors of impacted chewing gum, littered wrappers, diminishing puddles. She kept rolling the sleeves of her cardigan up and down, and watched her feet in their lemon-colored sneakers. Tammi had raspberry, and Jamie noticed how three paces of her sister's steps made up for one of her mother's, how worn her mother's sandals looked as they scuffed along the pavement. She remembered walking behind her mother at the beach once, fitting her own bare feet into the molds her mother's left in the wet sand. She wondered how many zillions of footprints had been left on Marine World's pavement—excited little kids, parents, maybe even some people like her spelling bee opponent Ricky who couldn't leave footprints because he was in a wheelchair. Feet moved on their own, she thought, beyond any will or awareness. She stopped, felt her body stretch forward and then pull back, a gentle yank as though she walked in cement that had instantly hardened. Everything hung, suspended, and then her mother turned around. "Jamie," was all her mother said, hair mussed and the smile she'd been carrying all day gone, for the indignation that had been building in Jamie all morning to flood her, deliciously. She sat down.

"What are you doing."

Jamie recognized the edge in her mother's voice. The pavement felt warm under her bottom. Tammi sang to her killer whale.

"I said. What. Are you doing."

Jamie closed her eyes to speak as precisely as if she were explaining to a doll. "I'm sitting down."

Tammi laughed, and their mother's hand reached out absently and rubbed her blond head. "Did you hurt yourself, Jamie? Did you have an accident?"

Jamie blew air out of her mouth, rolled her eyes. "No."

"Well," her mother said. "I thought something might be wrong." She picked up Tammi's hand. "We're going home now. Come on. Get up. Get in the car."

"I can't get in the car right now." Jamie was aware of passing shoes, passing strollers and pink blossoms of cotton candy and disembodied voices, the background to her private drama, a kind of blur. "The car is in the parking lot."

"Oh for chrissake," her mother said.

"You're not supposed to take the lord's name in vain," Jamie said. She had no idea what this meant, but she'd heard her grandmother say it once and had been impressed by its tone.

Her mother bent now, her voice a hiss. "This is getting tedious, Jamie. I can't believe you're acting this way. On your sister's birthday. You should be ashamed." She hitched her purse strap higher on her shoulder, hooked a lock of hair behind her ear, lowered her hand, snapped her fingers in Jamie's face. "Now."

Jamie shook her head, and her mother straightened up. "All right. Be that way." The woman who made up nicknames, who burned butter and milk, who held back Jamie's hair when she threw up, had vanished and in her place was a whitened face, a thin line of a mouth, eyes that did not tolerate nonsense. "Tammi and I are going home to have cake. You can get up and come with us or sit there and find your own way home. There are buses. You'll need to transfer but you're such a smart girl I'm sure you can figure it out."

She extended her hand to grab Tammi's sticky fist. The two of them walked away. Tammi looked back toward Jamie, who stared at the ground, and then their mother stopped. "*The car's in the parking lot,*" she mimicked in a hateful, scary voice. "See how far that attitude gets you. A smart-aleck, just like your father."

"It's your fault he's not here. It's your fault! If it wasn't for you he'd be here. He'd be here. He'd be here." Jamie's head began to shake, and she wiped her face. A family of five had grouped near the nearest bench, to pull children into sweaters and strollers, and stared at her. Jamie didn't care.

"Is that what you think?" And then her mother's voice changed, as if registering the way her whole body seemed to droop. "Oh, baby."

Tammi started to bawl then, and wrung her hand free of her mother's tight grasp. Her mother picked up Tammi and walked back to Jamie, a distance of about ten feet. "Now look what you've done." She sighed, wearily. "You've upset your sister."

"Good."

Jamie's mother's hand sprung out, slapped her cheek. Tears rose in Jamie's eyes but she made no expression. "If you didn't make me so mad," her mother began, and then turned and walked away, still carrying Tammi.

It looked like rain again, but Jamie wasn't worried. He'd show up sooner or later. Her mother hadn't given him half a chance.

Her mother and Tammi were smaller now, heading for the giant G underneath which they'd parked. Her mother had put on her white sweater. *Look back*, Jamie willed, but she couldn't see if even Tammi did because they kept getting smaller and then disappeared behind a black van. More and more people were streaming around Jamie now. "Lose your folks?" one lady asked, and Jamie didn't like the way her question sounded like it was supposed to be a joke. The family at the bench had moved on, and a man sat there alone, dark hair partially hiding his face, reading a brochure. Her heart leaped, and then fell as the man smiled at her. She stood up, primly straightening her dress, and frantically looked around. Outside the gate, their station wagon pulled up and Jamie ran toward it, her heart pounding.

BECAUSE SHE WAS FOUR NOW, TAMMI NO LONGER NEEDED HER car seat. And because it was her birthday, she got to sit shotgun, their mother called it, with a lecture on seat belts. Jamie sat alone in the back seat, and nobody said a word. When her mother made an early exit off the freeway and headed right instead of left, Jamie didn't ask why. Tammi was humming the theme song from Ophelia's show and playing with her stuffed killer whale, its smile stitched pink like a doll's.

"I think Tammi's had a happy birthday," her mother began, as if talking to the air. "Don't you?"

"Why don't you ask Tammi?"

Her mother's voice caught on the edge of irritation again, but stopped short. "Because it's you I'm worried about right now, Jamie." She reached her hand into her purse for a cigarette, which she lit as they drove down the frontage road.

Jamie slumped into the back seat, dress bunched around her bottom, underwear slicing into her thighs, and picked an old hardened scab on her knee. When the car pulled into the 7-Eleven parking lot, Jamie sat up to look at the group of men by the phones. She looked at their shoes, dirty leather boots and torn, soiled sneakers and beat-up old wingtips, and then up their legs and past reddened hands that hung loose at waists, around brown bags and hooked on belt loops, and to the faces. She made herself look at each one, but they were all strangers—weathered and wrinkled and unfamiliar. Jamie's mother walked right up to one of them, who pushed himself off from the wall where he'd been leaning against a raised foot and spoke to her.

"Tammi," Jamie whispered, "is this where you saw Daddy?"

Tammi looked out the window. "The daddy men," she confirmed.

Her mother got back in the car and drove out of the parking lot. Drizzle began as they crossed the overpass to the frontage road that ran next to the freeway. Jamie scanned both directions from the back seat windows, wanting to memorize everything about where they were going—the rushing freeway traffic, the sagging wire fence, the littered and puddled strip of dirt next to the fence, and, on the car's other side, squat stucco motels, pool halls, a nightclub with no windows and a marquee missing most of its letters. Her mother slowed the car to turn into a horseshoe driveway, drove around a patch of mud where a large bucket of tired geraniums sat below a large wooden wheel with painted lettering across its spokes that read *Wagon Wheel Motel,* and parked. She got out of the car, raising her sweater over her head like a cape, and walked into the office, where she spoke briefly with the man behind the counter and then walked out again and headed away from the car and toward one of the rooms. Jamie watched her knock on a door, and then turned away, slumped down, stared out the window at the gray sky and tops of trees and the weathered sign, two of its spokes broken, the white paint of the letters peeling off from the rain. *Wagon wheel.* What did the *h* add? The beginnings of both words felt the same in her mouth, pushing and pulling her lips.

She heard soft humming and popped up to see Tammi, straining at the seat belt to sit on her knees and swim her whale up toward the car light and dip it down again, like Ophelia's gymnastics at the opening of the Marine World commercial. Tammi dropped the whale then, and fell back down to the seat, and all Jamie could see was the crown of her sister's head, its tumble of blond curls so thick that Jamie drew her hand to her own head, to check the pencil-straight part she'd pulled through it that morning.

"Hey," she said, "you did have a happy birthday, didn't you?"

Tammi looked up, her smooth eyelids as uncreased as ripe peach skin, her face completely lacking in agenda, and Jamie felt puzzled, almost let down by knowing that her sister had gotten what she wanted. Then Tammi lifted the whale up to the window, and Jamie turned. There, on the other side of the car door, bending down with his hands on his thighs to look in the back seat window, he was.

"Daddy!" she shrieked, and grabbed the door handle. He pulled the door open, and she tumbled out of the car into his crouching embrace. Behind him, her mother turned in a little spin and stood with her back to the car, her arms crossed in front of her so her back in its white sweater looked narrow, hunched.

Jamie had never before considered her mother's vulnerability, and her awareness of it flared briefly before being snuffed out by her father's arms pulling her to his chest and then holding her by the shoulders to look into her face. Now that he was in front of her again, his features seemed both sharper and smaller, as if memory had not only blurred them but made him larger, and Jamie was a little stunned that this man holding her so tightly was just he. Just her father.

Tammi was butting her killer whale against the front seat window, calling "My whale, my whale, my whale," but when he moved his hand inside the car to touch her too, she slid down on the seat as if he were a stranger. "Happy birthday, little girl," he said then, tapping his fingers on her back. "Happy birthday." It was then that Jamie noticed that neither parent was making a move toward the driver's seat.

"Aren't you coming home with us?" Jamie asked. It wasn't raining hard, but drops blew in the open door and settled on her bare legs like spittle.

He glanced down, then briefly over his shoulder. "No, no, I can't."

He looked tired, Jamie thought, as if he'd just woken up. He kept rubbing his eyes.

"Why not?"

His hands dangled now in the space made by the V of his dirty jeans. "I just can't."

"Are you dying?"

He pulled back and snorted, as if he were going to laugh but changed his mind. "No. Not anytime soon," he said, and then as an afterthought, "As far as I know." He looked at her quickly, and then his pale blue eyes darted away again. "Why'd you think that?"

"You're sick, Mom said. That's why you left."

He shrugged, spoke softly: "Yes." His eyes looked sad now, but they met hers and did not look away. Jamie heard a car door open, and turned to see her mother get in the front seat and sit without moving, facing straight ahead. Jamie spoke quickly, words tumbling out before she'd thought of them. "Can I stay here with you? I don't have my p.j.s but we can go back and get them. My toothbrush and my homework and stuff. I can help you cook. I can stay for a while. Can't I?"

He shook his head and stood up, smoothing his hands down the front of his thighs. "No, no, that won't work, Jamelia."

His use of her old nickname made her feel embarrassed for him, the way she felt when new kids brought the wrong lunch boxes to school. He coughed into his fist, and then eased her into the back seat again and closed the door while Jamie rolled down its window, moved her face into the spray of rain.

"Maybe some other time," he said, nodding as if this was suddenly a good idea. "Yeah, some other time. Sometime soon. You all need to get back home now."

Tammi had stopped playing with the whale, and lay with her head in her mother's lap. Their mother didn't move, except for her hand slowly rubbing Tammi's back. They seemed in a different car, headed for a different destination. Jamie felt too full to go home with them to their apartment, where what was happening did not fit the life they'd left there that morning, the way she felt sometimes trying to get tidy, orderly letters to hold all the ways there were to make a sound.

Jamie looked at her father again, and when he raised his eyebrows the flatness lifted out of his eyes. She held her hand to the open space of the window, where his fingers were curled, and he fit his palm against and around hers.

"I'm the best speller in my class," she said. His eyes were glossy now. "I've won the last two bees and if I win the one next week, I'll be fourth grade champion."

"Fourth grade?"

"I'm two years ahead."

"That's real good. I'm proud of you."

"Were you a good speller?"

Her father coughed again, looked down, and when he looked up again, he drew his palm away, rubbed his neck. "Was I? I don't remember. I hated history and grammar, but I don't remember spelling. I might have been. Yeah, maybe I was. *I before E except after C.*"

"That's not always true. Science."

He tapped her hand with a pointed finger. "Ten points." He smiled now, and Jamie thought of the tricks with his lighter at the dinner table, the way he'd been in her memory, the way that would never change.

"You can help me practice my words sometime."

His eyes shifted again. "Sure. We'll see. I don't think I was a good speller. Your mom's better, I bet."

Her mother's voice startled Jamie, clear and loud from the front seat: "Jamie does it all herself. She's amazing." And then she started the car, and he stood up, stepped back. Her mother spoke again, this time leaning over Tammi to say out the front window, "Go to her bee, Walt, if you want to. It's up to you."

He nodded and winked at Jamie, but his smile faded quickly and he looked down again and turned away as the car backed up and pulled around the Wagon Wheel sign. Jamie watched him walk back into his room, and as the car sped up onto the frontage road, the air outside the window pressed against her lifted hand. She knew that she would always remember this place, and her limbs felt heavy. She watched the motel and pool hall and nightclub, the sagging fence and weedy strip of dirt recede behind the car. Then they crossed the overpass, and Jamie turned to lean forward between the front seat headrests. Tammi slept curled on the seat. Both of her mother's hands held the steering wheel, and Jamie believed she'd never get past this moment, never turn sixteen, never be able to turn the wheel as her mother was doing right now, moving the car past 7-Eleven as if she knew exactly what she was doing.

Falling

I AM BRUISING. AS I DRY MYSELF AFTER THE SHOWER WITH ONE foot and then the other up on the sink, as I pull socks on and later roll them off, I'm finding nickel- and dime-shaped bruises on my legs. They're not dramatic in terms of color—a pale, fleshy purple, a faint yellow tinge—but they hurt. This morning, there's one on my hip. I have no idea where it came from. Sometimes I walk into an open drawer at the library or bang against an open cupboard door, but the bruises I find have no correlation to any impact I remember.

Jeff says they result from some vitamin deficiency, I forget which, and if I eat more kelp and citrus, they'll go away. But I'm finding more and more of them. They can't just pop up unbidden, I ask, can they? They have to come from some meeting of skin and obstacle, some instance of what a doctor would call trauma. Jeff shrugs. "Some people just bruise more easily than others," he says, and kisses my knee. "It's nothing to worry about."

As a child, I loved Band-Aids. I loved the variety: small delicate rectangles with perfect gauze squares no bigger than a pinkie nail; big squares with fat gauze pillows in their center; bull's-eyes that looked like my grandmother's bunion pads. I loved the color, like Flesh in the Crayola box that matched the tone of no one's skin. I loved the medicinal smell, the metallic boxes, pulling the thin blue string so the crinkly paper would fall apart to reveal the bandage inside. I skinned my knees sliding down inclines of dirt and rock, climbing rough bark, skidding onto cement, and picked the scabs with secret, voluptuous pleasure. I went through box after box of Band-Aids, covering my skin even when there was nothing underneath to protect.

My father used to say injuries needed air to heal, needed to breathe. He used to say I should take off Band-Aids before the bath, but I left them on until they peeled off and floated to the top of the water. Then I lifted them, curled and sodden, to place on the edge of the tub. At the library, where every day I get at least two paper cuts from pulling papers out of files or—worse—from running a finger too quickly through the old card catalog drawers, I think of my father each time I wrap a small rectangular Band-Aid around the most recent, nearly invisible slit in my flesh.

•

I'm home at five o'clock when Adele calls to tell me the packet about literacy programs that I requested arrived in today's mail. I say I'll be right there and push back from the desk. It's so cluttered that Jeff's magazines, flagged with Post-Its, spill to the floor. I pick them up and move toward the coffee table, the couch, the TV, but every surface is littered with more photocopied articles and flagged books, so I place the magazines on the floor.

When Jeff and I moved to Bodega Bay two months ago, I
found part-time work at the Sebastopol public library, a half-
hour's drive away, and last month I sold an article to the *Pilot*,
the local paper, about Jeff's lab. It was a big hit, and Murray,
the *Pilot* editor, asked me to do another. "Get it to us by next
Friday," he said, "and maybe we can make this a regular thing."
Next Friday is a week away and I've been circling the same
vague, boring lead since three o'clock. I'm glad for a break.
The dog gets underfoot as I grab the keys from the hook
by the door. Jeff's had Jock, a big golden lab, since junior high.
I knew, when Jeff told me how he named the dog—after
Jacques Cousteau, host of Jeff's favorite TV specials, but with
a spelling more in keeping with Jeff's adolescent social priori-
ties—that this was a man I could love. Jock's slowing down,
grayer around the muzzle than when I first met him, and still
getting used to me. The other night he growled when I walked
in the kitchen. Jeff explained that Jock didn't know it was me
in the dark. Uh-huh, I said, what about the famous canine
sense of smell? It's the move, Jeff said then, he's never liked
change. I know how he feels.

"Back soon," I croon, bending down to see if he'll let me
scratch between his ears. His ears flatten, and I move my hand
away from his wet nose, close the door behind me.

It's been a wet day, and the March air is raw. Small yellow
flags dot the grass, snapping in the wind, marking boundaries
of one of Jeff's studies. All around are rampantly green
miner's lettuce and sourgrass, silvery blue lupine blossoms,
magenta-and-white flowering iceplant, California poppies
against a postcard backdrop of cliff and surf. Jeff's careful
attention to a foot-square plot of grasses seems so microscop-
ic, so focused, while I am distracted by the bay filling with
blue ocean at high tide, the fruit trees on Bodega Highway
puffing out with pink and white blossoms, the cows running
through the fields with such unsteadiness I feel a mild panic

at the sight of their big, low-slung bellies on spindly legs. Where are they headed and why, as they career, slightly out of control but wholly purposeful, down a sloping pasture? The red barn, the green grass, the black-and-white cows—it all seems too idyllic to be real.

• •

"I don't know if I have time to do this." I take the fat white envelope from Adele's hand. She's sitting behind the front desk, stamping in new periodicals. The library closes in forty-five minutes, and most of the afternoon patrons have left.

Adele arches an eyebrow.

"I mean, I really want to, but did I tell you? The *Pilot* wants another article."

"What are you going to write about this time?"

"What do you mean?"

"Your last one was all about the lab."

"I'm writing about the lab again. That's what they're interested in."

Adele peers at me. I've seen her intimidate adults with this look: Are you sure you mean *Charlotte* Brontë? Do you *really* know what you're looking for? Her eyes are brown with flecks of gold. I'm not up to their demands.

I shrug, and swat the envelope against my hand. Its metered postage is neat on the clean white paper, my name typed below on a printed label. "Anyway, Jeff and I are going to Woods Hole in June, he has a two-month research fellowship there. How much could I get off the ground before then?"

She moves the magazines aside, smooths her wool skirt over her lap, leans forward. "Let's take a look."

"I can't right now, I have to get back."

Adele nods, and something she won't say out loud is thrown into the upward tilt of her chin, her pursed lips, her glittering eyes. She's never met Jeff, but I can tell she doesn't like him.

"I'll see you tomorrow. Thanks." I wave the envelope and head out the door.

• • •

The Tidewater is lighting up, the neon beer sign in the window reflecting off the water below in a pink smear. It's started to rain again, and the wet road gleams in the shine of headlights. I park the car and walk to the edge of the parking lot. To the east, the sky is gunmetal above hills that seem a preternatural green, but past the mouth of the bay where Bodega Head looms, the lowering sun gilds the bellies of swollen clouds.

The bar is dim, as always: sunset kept out by green plastic window shades, dark paneled walls draped with fish nets cradling dusty, colored-glass balls, yellowed buoys, life pre-servers with twisted, fraying cords. Paul pours me a beer from the pitcher as I slide into the empty chair next to Jeff. There are four of us tonight, at our usual corner table. I'm getting used to these Friday nights at the Tidewater, to the way the others don't stop talking when I sit down.

"At least Andy gave her time off," Paul is saying.

"It's the least he could do," Margo answers.

I put a hand on Jeff's thigh and lean toward his ear. "Hi," I whisper into his thick blond hair. He covers my hand with his own and speaks across the table to Margo.

"It's a tough deal," he says. "You want to be sympathetic, but you've got a real serious deadline. Andy's in a bind. Elaine's compiled that data, she knows it better than anyone."

"Those are her urchins," Paul says and smiles, as if he's said something funny.

"And her dad just died." Margo's hands rest on top of a beer mug, one layered over the other like white petals.

"It's going to take Andy three times as long to get that grant application in without her here," Jeff says. "She knows that stuff backwards and forwards. She could probably recite it in her sleep."

"When's the application due? A week from Monday?" I ask, thinking of the mess at home, Jeff's papers covering everything.

"The grant can wait." Margo stares at me.

"It's tough," Jeff says again. And then, "But it really can't wait." His smile means he's merely being realistic. "We're talking about twenty thousand dollars. That's a large percentage of those urchins' operating costs."

"Andy's a hero," Paul says, pouring more beer in his glass. Margo peels her hands off hers and he tops it off, too. "He'll get it done."

"It's hardly heroism," Margo says. "Jesus. It's the least he can do." Her hands encircle the beer mug now, palms against beveled glass, and she leans farther over the table, her eyes on Jeff.

I start talking before she covers her glass again. "When my father died, my uncle drove back and forth seventy miles to get my brother and me to school so my mom didn't have to. He did it every day for two weeks." Uncle Joe's big ex-football player body hunched into the driver's seat of my mom's Pacer. He packed us sack lunches of HoHos and Saltines spread with peanut butter until Mom found out and told him to put in an apple too. "It's funny what you remember," I say, although I haven't thought of this in years.

"When was that?" Paul asks.

"Twelve years ago last month. February sixth. I remember Bugs Bunny was on TV in the waiting room when the nurse came to get us. That nurse was big and intimidating, always shooing my brother and me around. She started to fiddle with some stuff by the bed, I don't know what, unhooking a monitor or something. My mother told her to get out. I was impressed. She left, and we stood there a while. My father looked the same, just sleeping. He'd been sick for so long."

Jeff's hand is still in mine, and he's sitting back a bit, giving me a look I recognize from our first week here, when I glanced up from loading the washer one day to see him standing in the doorway. "Why are you staring at me like that?" I asked. He came up, put his arms around me. "It's you," he said. "I love watching you alone, like I'm spying through a one-way mirror." I teased him for a while—"You want to watch me sort the darks?"—but it scared me a little, too.

No one says anything. Behind Margo's head, a wire spiderweb divides the dartboard into chunky black and red plots. Numbers circle the periphery. I have no idea what they mean.

• • • •

It's pouring when we leave, so Jeff and I run to the car and climb in quickly. I tell him we're lucky to be having another wet winter after a long drought, but he doesn't answer. He's not one to talk while driving in heavy rain. We pull into the driveway and he jerks up the emergency brake. "Why didn't you ever tell me that before?"

"What?"

"About your father."

My father died a slow death, and I've told Jeff about the hospital bed set up in our living room, my father growing paler and thinner, patting the sheet for me to sit beside him after school and tell him what I'd done that day. Sometimes I'd come home to find the apartment quiet and a note on the kitchen table, and I'd know he'd been readmitted. Those nights, my brother and I knew to heat up a can of soup or Spaghetti-Os, not to wait up for our mom.

"You knew my father died."

He is working his hands against the steering wheel. "Yes, but I didn't know your uncle drove you and Billy to school for two weeks. I didn't know you saw him after he passed away."

I touch the door handle. "I was only eleven, you know. Billy was thirteen. Some people might say my mother was wrong, letting us see him."

"You think so?"

"I don't know. People say a lot of stupid things about death." Rain falls like darting needles onto the hood of the car, and in the glow from the kitchen light—we always leave it on for Jock—the drops bounce and skitter, falling too fast to pool. "What's with Margo, anyway?"

"She's just upset about Elaine. Why'd you have to say all that in front of her. In front of Paul." He shakes his head.

"It just came out, Jeff. It's not like I've been hiding it from you."

"Well, it felt that way. We're talking about the grant and then—" His hands fly off the steering wheel as if it were suddenly electrified, and then he sighs, and they fall into his lap.

I shrug, lean my head back. He cups my neck in his warm palm, stroking the skin behind my ear. I feel my earring sway, the small round weight of its agate stone.

"I keep thinking of Elaine, taking a whole week off from work. My dad died late in the day. We had the funeral and scattered his ashes on a weekend. I didn't miss a day of school." I can feel Jeff's eyes watching me. "Everyone kept saying 'Time will make it better.' I wanted them all to go away. I felt like it was a trick. I didn't get it." I stare at the ripped sun guard, its torn vinyl, its exposed yellow foam. "I still don't."

But then I think of something, and when I shake my head, the hairs that have worked themselves loose from my barrette pull against Jeff's fingers.

"What?" he asks. Rain drums on the car roof.

"Please"—my voice surprises me, loud in the foggy car— "don't say passed away." I pull the handle to open the door. "He died."

But that's not it. I wanted to see his eyes, I remember now; I asked my mother if they could open. And although I can still see his face as clearly as I did that day in the hospital, the features that were undeniably his, I cannot remember the exact color of his eyes.

•   •   •   •   •

With Elaine out of town, Jeff feeds the urchins on the weekend. I go with him to stand at the tanks and toss in plugs of brown food that come apart like sawdust when they hit the water. "Far Side" cartoons stud the hallway walls, and I buy M&Ms and a Diet Coke from vending machines in a dank, windowless room. I love the lab. The smell of chemicals, the square signs warning of radioactivity, the damp cement floor sloping down to circular drains, the big round tanks filled with ink-purple sea urchins and masses of brine shrimp, the yellowish square tanks filled with water and algae and specimens, cordlike tubes running in and out. Cards list the names of the researchers and the projects, the estimated completion date of the experiment usually a casually penciled question mark. Saline content, oxygen, nitrogen, hydrogen—all carefully measured and monitored, the water level kept regular and sufficient, yet the end result is unknown. Not even a date with "approx." or "circa." Just a blatant, unapologetic question mark. The lab is set up for control, for plottable, incremental change, and I am in love with the question marks, marking the tanks like SOS flags.

• • • • • •

At night, in bed, I reach for Jeff. His solidity, the coarse texture of his hair in my hands, the thickness of his chest under my cheek, comfort me. He holds me, and as I begin to drift off, I feel his touch change, his hands moving between my legs, onto my breasts, and I fake sleep, roll out of reach. Until recently I slept on my back, arms outstretched, or curled toward him, my breasts pressed against his shoulder blades, my pubic hair brushing his lower back. I remember waiting for him while he brushed his teeth, throwing my legs around him, pulling off his underwear with my toes, rocking into him as if I were the curved base and he a hobby horse. I remember crying out to him, grabbing his hair, biting his shoulder; I remember sex so good I fell asleep for twelve hours afterward and did not move from where I'd fallen, on top of his arm; the whole next day something rippled in me every-time my skin was touched, even if it was a metal doorknob against my hand. I remember these things as if they happened to another woman.

• • • • • • •

Adele tells me one reason she's so pleased with my work is that I find things to do without being asked. After the Monday morning rush and before school lets out, I pick up magazines from tables and chairs and return them to their metal shelves; I wrap sheets of plastic around new hardcovers, tucking each corner securely; I sort tax forms and refill the cartons on top of the card catalog with small, pointy pencils.

When Jeff's at home, even if he's plugged into his Diskman and huddled over the desk, he fills up the house in a way that takes my attention, my mind, and tethers it to him. I've inter-viewed Andy and Margo, studied Elaine's graphs of sea urchin colonization rates, but when I sit at the table and stare at my notes, I'm too aware of Jeff's breathing, the tattoo of his pencil, the thick blond back of his head. I put down my pen to do the dishes or a load of laundry, telling myself I need some distance, telling myself something will come to me when I'm at the library, where my mind is my own again. But nothing does. I look up to see a boy standing in front of the magazines. I didn't even hear the automatic doors open. He picks up *Mad* and then *Life*, and when he passes over *Sports Illustrated*, I know he isn't avoiding a homework assignment. After a few minutes, he's sitting against the wall, a book open against his thighs, reading. I push the cart over and bend next to him to check a call number. The open page on his lap is covered with two columns of type, no pictures. His wrists are thin and pale out of his gray sweatshirt sleeves, and he wears glasses. Ten, I think, or maybe eleven; is that too young for his classmates to call him a nerd? A bookworm, I think, our library doing its purpose. I smile at the mussed top of his head. As I move around the library, reshelving books, I look up from time to time and he is still there.

A group of seventh-graders tramps in at 3:45, and Adele and I are both at the front desk, answering questions—Who was Clara Barton? Why aren't there any books with color pictures of the Civil War?—for the rest of the afternoon. When they check out, I like to look at each child and say something about his or her subject—Cats or Rare Gems or Dinosaurs—but today their faces run together behind a steady stream of books. A stack appears on the desk, lifted by narrow pale hands, five or six books on astronomy and a biography of Edmund Halley. This kid knows his way around: Biography is on the opposite end of the library from Science, so he couldn't have found the Halley book side by side with the others. It's my boy, looking up at me with head tilted back and eyes magnified by his glasses. I smile and say, "Enjoy your books, come back soon," but he doesn't respond, and I watch him walk out the door, stiff denim pants hanging loose over thin hips and flat buttocks. In profile, his glasses look too large for his face, and I want to push them back from where they have slid, halfway down his nose.

• • • • • • • •

When my father was well, we went on frequent outings to Monterey Bay, to Mount Tam, to the Mendocino dunes, to the Marin Headlands, to see tidal pools, to watch migrating whales, to hike bluffs and ridges and hold our breath through the tunnel on the way to Fort Cronkhite's pebbly beach. My father taught medical research at UCSF, but watching him turn over a leaf gently with a stick to show us a grub clinging underneath, I thought he knew about everything. One morning, after we spent the night at Sky Camp in Point Reyes, he stopped on the trail back to the parking lot, his arms in the air and a radiant smile on his face, at the sight of sunshine shafting through the redwoods, lighting up scores of spider webs hanging from branches like coins on a charm bracelet.

These outings grew less frequent when my father got sick, and then stopped altogether, and nature became science, the dry lifeless stuff of crackly-skinned, Formaldehyde-drenched frogs and faded and torn Periodic Charts. I didn't visit those places again until Jeff and I met and he took me to Point Reyes and Muir Woods to hike trails I didn't recognize, where he identified native species of grasses and birds, followed by dinners in Olema or Sausalito. From the beginning, Jeff's calm manner and knowledge soothed me. His clear sense of where he's headed has made it easy to follow along, as if his shadow cast a glow as purposeful as his stride.

• • • • • • • •

"A kid came in today and checked out a bunch of astronomy books, and it gave me an idea."

"Mm. What's that?" Jeff stands at the kitchen counter, elbow bent at his side, wrist and hand circling rapidly as he whisks a thin thread of olive oil into a bowl. He makes salad dressing every night, but pours his over iceberg lettuce. I still can't believe that someone so knowledgeable about plants—their varieties, their permutations—would be so devoted to iceberg lettuce. He says it's because he grew up on it, it's mother food, comfort food. He's the only person I know who considers lettuce comfort food. To me, iceberg lettuce is no more than water, water with crunch, but he likes that crunch, says lettuce should be crisp, refreshing, not limp and droopy like the gourmet varieties I buy for myself at farmers' stands along Bodega Highway. It's our only domestic difference.

I look at him from where I stand, chopping zucchini. "You and some of the guys from the lab—Andy, maybe Margo and Elaine—could come give a nature talk. You could bring in some plants, an anemone or two. Tell some good bug reproduction stories."

He is leaning into the counter now, poking around the small pots of herbs on the windowsill. "Don't we have dill?"

"I think so. Look in the cupboard."

On the refrigerator we keep a magnetized clip holding a pad of white paper. He picks up the stubby pencil next to the phone and writes, in his small neat hand so suited to chemical formulas and long strings of numbers, FRESH DILL.

I push the zucchini slices into a bowl with the edge of the knife and start on the eggplant. "So? Do you like my idea?"

"Oh, I don't know, Kit. We're so strapped these days, with the grant application due in a week and Elaine out, we can barely remember to eat lunch. Besides, I don't know if the research we're doing now would interest kids. Urchins and grasses can't compare to Super Mario Brothers."

"They could if you made them fun. You were ten once too, you know. You would've loved an event like that—getting out of class, torturing specimens."

"If you could've torn me away from Ace Comics." He grins. "Beat a day in nature any time."

We work silently, the knife in my hand now sliding easily through the firm flesh of fresh mushrooms, his hands tearing lettuce under running water. Jock lies against the stove, tail thumping, head drooped on his paws, eyes on Jeff.

"This kid who came in today, checked out astronomy books, I wanted to do more than just stamp his book on Halley's Comet with a due date."

"We don't have materials to talk about astronomy."

"I know, Jeff, it's the general idea I'm talking about. Use a little imagination." *For once*, I think, and turn on the flame beneath a heavy pan. Jock lifts his head, ears alert. My face feels warm, and I continue, softer now, "Exciting kids about nature, about science. Do they even know miner's lettuce is edible? Does anyone eat sourgrass anymore?"

"I hope not. Dogs piss on it." Jeff bangs the wooden servers against the salad bowl and carries it to the table. Our landlady left a lot of nice things for us in the kitchen: a salad bowl with matching servers, a set of handpainted mugs and plates, even a coffee machine and a food processor, heavy seasoned cast-iron pans that hang over the stove. We took the place furnished, and at first, it was the best kind of playing house. All the props were already here. We barely had to unpack. Our stuff sits in the garage with the bicycles and the washer/dryer.

Jeff's leaning against the sink now, arms crossed, watching me pour oil into the pan. It skips spitting across the hot iron surface, and I spill in the vegetables. "We're just not set up to do outreach to the schools. Besides, we already have the visitor's center," he says. The marine center stays open to the public two days a week from ten to noon, and mounted displays along its hallways show everything from whale migration patterns to the life cycle of starfish.

"That's hardly community outreach."

"We're primarily research, not education." He taps his palms against the counter. "How's the article coming along? Andy said he gave you more information over the phone."

"It's not." The vegetables are sizzling in the hot pan. I reach into the cupboard next to the stove and pull out the sesame oil. "Coming along," I add, opening the bottle and drizzling some over the mushrooms, the zucchini, the eggplant.

"What are you doing?"

"I just bought this today, it has a good flavor."

"Kit, you know I'm allergic to sesame seeds."

"Oh, god." I lift the pan off the flame and step quickly to the sink, dump the vegetables with a twist of my wrist, hot oil hissing and steaming against the wet basin, Jeff shouting, "Don't! Kit, c'mon," reaching for my arm, and the pan clatters out of my hand and into the porcelain sink, making a racket so Jock jumps up, ears cocked, nails clicking on the linoleum, barks once. My hands, empty now, throbbing, reach up to my wet cheeks and make fists I push my face into.

"Hey, hey, hey," Jeff says, drawing me to him, pulling my hands open to blow on them. He turns on the water and holds my palms under the faucet, fingers tight on my wrists. "Jesus, Kit, what's going on?" Jock whimpers and nuzzles our ankles, so all I can do for an answer is stand there, caught at hands and feet, trapped and comforted at the same time.

• • • • • • • • •

Fatigue weighs on my shoulders, my eyelids, my feet. I stare at my notes, but they make no sense. I am trapped in stuffy heat, in my own dense mind. I've already eaten lunch and fed Jock and watered the primulas and herbs and drunk a cup of coffee. It's 2:14. The article is due in three days. My mind keeps skipping like a broken record back to the reminder that I have to be at the library tomorrow and Thursday mornings, that I have to write something today.

But this table is too low. My upper body has to tilt too far forward; my neck is a stem that can't hold up the bobbing, fat bud of my head. I close my eyes to the living room wall and imagine the soft, quick clicking of fingers on a keyboard, the gurgle and churn of tanks and filters, the constant productivity of swimming pulsing alive things. I leave my notes, which trail into tiny, unreadable scrawl, and walk over to the couch to dream of the creatures in Jeff's lab, suckers and pinchers and feelers dancing together in clear, constantly splashing, aerated water.

• • • • • • • • •

Adele listens to me, her eyes steady on my face, spooning up lemon yogurt from a carton. "Of course you know enough to give a nature talk," she says. "Forget those inflated egos at the lab; they'll speak over the children's heads anyway. You have enthusiasm and energy, Kit. That's the most important thing. The rest, well, you can look it up. This is a library, after all."

I stare at her. "But I can't even get the article written."

"So? You'll write it. Then you can think about nature talks. You could do hikes, too." Behind the library is a field with a creek, high and fast with run-off, banks lush with miner's lettuce. She leans forward, ruffles through her Page-a-Day, taps next Thursday with her finger. "Two fifth-grade classes are coming in next week from Emerson elementary, you could do something then."

Imagined, my idea was inviolate; now that Adele has made it sound possible, it doesn't feel like mine anymore. "It's too much. I can't deal with it right now. I can't even think past Friday."

She looks up at me, cleans the spoon between closed lips. "Have you read that packet from San Rafael?"

"I looked at it the other night." She will run away with this too, I think, but I keep talking. "They hold three workshops a year. There's one that starts in two weeks, and another in June."

She nods. "We could spare you in June."

"I won't even be here in June."

She puts down the carton of yogurt. "Why did you move to Bodega Bay?"

"Jeff got this great lab appointment, post-doc, for two years—"

"Why did you move to Bodega Bay?" she repeats, and we are both silent until I say quietly, "Because I love Jeff."

I hate her for the prissy defensiveness I hear in my voice. I pick up the envelopes she's piled neatly for today's mail, and turn to the door. My voice is brisk now: "Look Adele, I appreciate your concern, your advice, but I can't handle switching gears now. The *Pilot's* counting on me. So is the lab."

"Forget the lab, Kit. It's not yours."

I walk away.

• • • • • • • • • •

I am groggy, heavy with sleep as if drugged. I think of my arm, my leg, but they are apart from me, too heavy to lift, even to move. "What are you doing?" I hear myself murmur, the words like marbles. He is on top of me, moving, then rigid, and as I open my eyes, he relaxes and falls onto my chest, my thighs. I am smothered.

"Hey," he says, his breath raggedy.

"I was asleep." My mouth feels numbed.

"Yeah? You sure fooled me." He traces my nipple with his thumb.

"When did you get home?"

"A little while ago."

I start to cry.

His hand moves off my breast. "I really didn't know."

I shake my head and pull hair out of my mouth.

"It's something else, isn't it." His voice is gentle but the weight of his body still presses down. "Don't worry," he whispers. "I'm not going anywhere."

I lift my head, but all I see is the shadow of his shoulders. I am glad for the dark, glad that I can keep him from seeing in my face that that is not it at all. He rolls off me and I lean my head on his chest and sob, as if I can have this part of him and nothing else.

• • • • • • • • •

I'm home early from work on Thursday, and after I let out the dog and eat lunch, I put on my jacket, grab Jock's leash and open the door, call to him. "Going for a walk," I say, "you want to come?" He sniffs along the driveway, then looks at me as if changing his mind and slinks past my legs back into the house. "Fine," I say, closing the door, "be that way."

The sky is heavy with dark clouds but when the sun shines though intermittently, the iceplant looks frosty, as if morning dew were still on it. Lupine branches are as dark green as Christmas trees, and manzanita bark gleams dark, glossy red. Poppies flutter their orange petals like flags, some still tightly furled. I walk toward one of Jeff's plots—indistinct grasses pulling up from the ground. Some blades are bent and brown, flattened against the moist earth by rain or deer, and I find their collapse both touching and accusatory, a reminder of what is vulnerable and sweet in Jeff.

Back at the house, Jock is sitting where I left him, just inside the door. "Okay, we're even," I say. "Come on." He follows me this time, down the road to the beach. Behind the lab, on the other side of the faultline, the bushy vegetation abruptly ends, and the land becomes hilly and sparse with beachgrass whose color shifts in the wind, showing green when pressed flat and shining gold when rising up again. I unclip Jock's leash and he takes off, running, sand lifting behind him in a cloud. I press into the dunes with the toes of my sneakers, tilt my body forward, and climb.

At the top of the dunes, the Pacific stretches before me its endless, swelling gray carpet, broken only by a white line of surf and, on the horizon, a fishing boat tracking slowly southward. I stood at the side of a boat like that once, gripping its ropes in my fisted hands, watching my uncle pour my father's ashes into dark water. It was cold, I remember, a damp, windy day. I remember the barking of seals, the stink of low tide, the crust of barnacles revealed on the dock.

•   •   •   •   •   •   •   •

One summer night, my father took me to a field, a short walk from the cabin my parents had rented on the Russian River. It was the latest I'd ever been allowed to stay up, and my father had carried a blanket so that we could lie down, heads touching, and watch the sky. It must've been before he was sick, because I was only five, but I remember being scared that his feet were so far away, off the edge of the blanket, sticking up from bare ankles like abandoned, upended toy boats, and he wiggled them to show that they were still connected to him. His sandy hair fell down into his collar and swooped low over his forehead, and his face with its long, thin nose and ginger-colored hornrimmed glasses stared straight overhead. We were watching for falling stars, he told me. I wanted to catch one, I wanted one to land right next to us, a glowing white globe settling on the empty field where I imagined it would light up our faces like a bonfire.

He told me how constellations seem to change position in the sky because of the earth's rotation, how falling stars aren't really stars at all but junk in the atmosphere. And then, as he later told the story, one fell.

"There's one!" he said. "Look at that!"

"That's a falling star," I said, and I felt it in my gut, the way I would later feel my first roller coaster, my first take-off in a small plane, the first brush of my breasts against Jeff's bare chest.

"That's what we call it. A meteor."

"It moved. Falling is a kind of moving."

My father would repeat my words again and again in the years before he died, and I know they came from that night, from the first of what would be several hours of meteor showers. I remember the soft flannel of the blanket under my skin and the way lights would stream across the sky, suddenly, without warning. The next few nights I insisted on leaving my bedroom window open the whole way, so one might fall in by my bed.

•   •   •   •   •   •   •

I sit at the desk and pull the fat packet out from where I've tucked it in the bookshelves, between the dictionary and the Peterson's guides. Jeff was up and out before I was even awake, taking most of the mess of papers and books with him, and I shove what's left out of my way. Jock saunters over as if it's no big deal and curls at my feet, and I push my bare toes under his warm barrel belly. Outside it's raining again, and so dark I don't even notice as four o'clock becomes five and then six. I keep reading, making notes and imagining myself at a table in the back room of the library, with books and slides and piles of crayons and pads of paper, young faces shining eagerly up at me.

When I get up to feed the dog and rustle up some dinner for myself, I know what to do. Murray's in a late meeting at the *Pilot*, but I leave a message and he calls me back in ten minutes. I tell him I can't finish the article. I tell him I'm sorry to let him down. I tell him I will leave my notes with the lab for fact-checking and if they want to pursue the article with another writer, they can call Jeff.

• • • • • • •

Mrs. Carlyle comes in the library this morning, as she does every Friday, leaning on the arm of her companion, a volunteer at the residence home where Mrs. Carlyle lives. The volunteer heads for Recent Periodicals, and Mrs. Carlyle walks over to the card catalog, where her gnarled, arthritic hands pull out a drawer and worry slowly through its cards.

Mrs. Carlyle is fascinated by the lives of politicians, but seems to have no organizing scheme, no overriding nationality or particular decade or century of focus. I've checked out books to her on Disraeli, Jefferson, Sun Yat-Sen. Today, as I place a recently published compilation of Lincoln's speeches her companion has handed me into the return bin, and stamp the due date into a biography on Churchill's early years in Parliament, I ask Mrs. Carlyle if she's comparing the two politicians, both so famous for their speeches, their moral leadership in times of national crisis. "Oh, my goodness, no," she says. "I just like them both." That seems a good enough reason, and categorization beyond taste seems suddenly arbitrary and foolish.

• • • • • •

Saturday morning is clear and sunny. I have showered, dressed, and eaten, and am debating leaving a note for Jeff when he opens the kitchen door, whistling. It's the first time I've seen him in two days. Jock trots in past him, panting and squirmy, and noisily laps water from his metal bowl.

"Beautiful morning." Jeff kicks his boots against the outside of the door jamb. This is when I've always loved him most, back from his birdwatching, damp from dew and perspiration, cheeks flushed and full of excitement over what he's seen. "Saw a redtail and three sparrow hawks."

"Good." Without the extra five minutes I stayed in bed, I'd be gone by now. "You guys done?"

"In the home stretch." He raises his eyebrows. "You're up early."

"Yeah, I have to go to the library. Adele's decided it's time to clean out the files, and she's promised me donuts and cappuccino if I help her." I hadn't planned to lie.

He unbuckles his fanny pack, with its notebook and pencil, its folded Ziploc bags, and places it on the counter. He moves toward me. His wrists are thick, his chest blocks the light from the window. "I was hoping you'd still be in bed." His lips touch the back of my neck, his hands go around my waist. "Thought I might make up for the other night."

I move quickly, slide toward the sink to rinse out my coffee mug. "I've got to get going."

There is hardly any traffic, and in another hour I am crossing the Golden Gate. I drive to the apartment building where I lived as a child, before my father got sick and couldn't climb stairs. The building's been painted, although I can't remember the original color. I can't even remember if we had a third or fourth floor apartment; I just remember it was the corner unit. I remember my room, a scratchy brown carpet with a hole cut in it for the heating vent. I remember my father's footsteps on the hardwood floors, a loose board in the hallway outside the bathroom, glass-fronted cupboards in the kitchen where my mother kept her prettiest dishes. I remember the four plastic cups lined up on the shelf next to the bathroom sink, yellow, pink, green, and blue, one with a water-stained razor handle sticking from it. I remember the view from the bay windows in the living room, across the street and over the roofs of pastel stucco buildings to the wind-warped cypresses in Lincoln Park, two blocks away. My father took us there to fly kites and look for salamanders under logs. I brought one home in a mayonnaise jar with holes poked in the lid, but touched it so much it dried out. Mostly we found a lot of golf balls.

I drive back through the Presidio toward the bay. I remember a short-cut, but get trapped going the wrong way and find myself approaching the Golden Gate Bridge at sixty miles an hour. I slow the car, and pull into the parking lot before the toll plaza. I get out and lock the car.

It's cold and windy on the bridge, my eyes tearing so much I can't see clearly, my hair whipping around my face. I once read that most suicides jump over the east side of the bridge, into the bay, rather than over the west, and supposed this was because the ocean and infinity were too bleak even for them. Now I wonder if it's because the west side is harder to get to by foot. I want to be over there, on the ocean side. I stare seaward across the rushing tops of cars, and think of the ashes scattered on the water twelve years ago, falling apart as they landed.

My father knew that meteors flare brightly and fantastically in our little corner of the sky, and only seem to plummet to nothing, and he must have known he was leaving himself all around me, on the land and in the sky as much as in this dark water. Nobody can live up to that, nobody alive, nobody I'd want.

He's gone, but he's here now speaking to me, healthy as he once was, his voice quick and happy as I stood in my nightgown and listened to him talking on the phone. My feet, I remember now, my feet on the cold hardwood floor, watching to avoid the board that squeaked when stepped on. *Listen to this, Mel, you've got to hear what Kit said: She said, Stars move, she said Falling is a kind of moving. God,* he said, *god I love that kid.*

• • • • •

The next day, I wait until five to set the table. I toss the salad made from three kinds of lettuce. I do the dishes, uncork the wine to let it breathe. I shower and wash my hair. The bathroom is still steamy as I wipe off the sink and put out a clean hand towel. I pull my damp hair back with a large clip Jeff calls the shark's jaw, and put on my favorite slouchy dress—rayon, with a dropped waist and a bright splashy floral pattern. Elaine and Margo and Andy and Paul are due at 6:30 to celebrate the completion of the grant application.

At 6:20, Jeff still isn't home. I look at the list, clipped to the refrigerator magnet, that we made together this morning, counting back from a dining time of 7:15. The chicken is in the oven, roasting; I baste it again. I have taken the carrot soup out of the refrigerator to bring it to room temperature before heating it. I have tied chives into little bouquets, bruising the green blades in my fingers, to place on top of each bowl. I study the writing on the list; Jeff's small letters look sloppier than usual, his printed all caps falling to lower case and running together in a few places to a ligatured *fi*, an *r* that is part of its preceding *a*. The letters shift slightly, as if they are gelling, and come to rest around the words "Prepare salad first." With the same shock I felt when I first saw my eyebrows on my mother's face, the same tall rabbity space between upper lip and nose, I recognize my *fi*, my *ar*. I wrote the list.

He walks in as I'm wiping the kitchen counter one more time. "Hi."

"Glad you could make it."

"I had to check everything one more time." He's bending over to unlace his shoes. His blond hair is lighter at the tips and darker, almost greenish, at the crown.

"Elaine's back, you said. You guys finished the application. You said."

He drops his muddy shoes outside the front door and nods. "I just wanted to check the numbers again."

"Hadn't they already been checked?"

"Not by me."

The skin on my hand pulls over my knuckles as I squeeze the sponge into the sink. "Does Elaine know you were checking up on her?"

"You make it sound like I'm the enemy." He shakes his head, and I see his eyes focus on the clock on the wall behind me. "I've got to get changed." But he doesn't move.

"What would you have done if they hadn't added up?"

He shrugs. "Luckily I don't have to consider that. They did."

"Well, then, why? Why drive yourself nuts checking something it's too late to do anything about?"

"I'm not nuts. It makes me feel better, calmer. I know the numbers are okay now. You're the one who's upset. Look at you: you're about to jump out of your skin."

"You know what? I'd like it better if you were nuts. If you were a nervous wreck about this grant. Anxiety is human."

"How do you know I wasn't anxious? Elaine just got back, we had to work two all-nighters. You know damn well it's been crazy."

"Jeff, her father just died."

"I know. That's what I'm saying. Her emotions could've gotten in the way of her work."

"Oh, please. Your work could get in the way of your emotions."

"What the hell do you know about my emotions these days?" His skin burns easily, and his face is mottled now with red and white as if he wore sunscreen that failed in patches. He opens his mouth as if to say something more, but instead, shaking his head again, turns and walks away.

I suck in my breath and lean back against the counter, my hands on my cheeks. Headlights shine across the kitchen window. Jock rises to his feet with clicking paws and a short bark, and I listen to a slamming car door and the crunch of feet on gravel. Options fly wildly to me—a sudden attack of cramps, the flu, a dramatic fainting fall on the linoleum floor—but I realize I am relieved by the prospect of other people. By the time they've left, Jeff's and my words will no longer have the immediacy they do now, and we'll pretend they don't exist, so they'll sit like our boxes in the garage, neglected and dusty but as bulky and dark as ever.

• • • •

Jeff is an adept host, filling wine glasses and chatting pleasantly with Elaine on his right and Margo on his left. Everyone praises the food. Margo says she has never seen poached pears outside of *Gourmet* magazine. Elaine lifts her glass slowly, and Paul, drunk already, loose and sloshy the way he always gets at the Tidewater, rings his knife against his glass so that we all look her way.

"Thanks to all of you for helping out, for covering me. It made a big difference." Her eyes are shiny with tears, and I feel my own throat constrict. I'm glad nobody says anything. "Kit, you too, even though you're not at the lab—"

"Even though you didn't do anything," Paul says, and chuckles.

"I made dinner," I say.

Margo is leaning forward, looking at Paul, "Yes, she did," and then, to me, says, "Your article was really helpful."

"Here's to Kit." Paul raises his glass, and dark wine presses against the swell of goblet, leaving a wash of blood, burgundy slime.

"Here's to no more all-nighters." Margo lifts her class.

"For now," Paul says.

"It's just too bad we couldn't get your next article in there too," Andy tells me, but his eyes are kind.

"I'm glad it was helpful," I say, and take a sip of wine. It is one way to get my mouth out of the smile it has frozen into.

Jeff and I offer seconds and pour more wine, clear the dinner plates and stack them in the sink, serve dessert, don't look at each other. After dessert we turn on the stereo and play Big Band music, opening more wine and pushing the empty bottles to the center of the table. We roll back the rag rugs and dance in our socks. Jock lies in front of the bathroom door, panting proprietarily. Jeff leaves the room for a moment and returns with the guitar I haven't seen him play since we moved here, and strums songs from childhood as the rest of us sprawl on the couch and floor. "Puff the Magic Dragon," we sing, and "American Pie" and "Horse with No Name." Was Puff really marijuana, Paul asks, and we all laugh. No, really, he says, insistent. Think of what happens with little Johnny Paper.

• • •

When I walk into the library on Monday morning, Adele is scanning returns into the computer. She looks up at me with her cocked eyebrows; I wonder why she wears an expression of what is, for her, surprise, and then I feel the smile on my own face.

"Is it okay if I change my schedule, start working full days Wednesday, Thursday, Friday?"

"I suppose. Why?"

"I'm going to go to San Rafael tomorrow. I want to talk to some people, see what I can find out about their after-school programs. I spoke to one of their head librarians on Friday, and she said there's room in the training workshop that starts next week. Every Monday for seven hours for four weeks. And then maybe—with yours and Raymond's approval—I could start something here."

She puts down the scanning wand, lifts a stacks of books onto the reshelving cart. "You know this means staying through the summer."

"If I decide to do it."

Her head goes back, watching me. "Right." She presses her hand, dry and silky from years spent touching paper, on my arm, and gets up, gestures to the computer screen. "All yours. I'm going in back to catch up on invoices."

I sit down and get to work.

• •

The front door slams, followed by the drop of shoes, the slurp of Jock at his bowl, a questioning "Hey!"

"In here," I call.

He fills the bedroom doorway, leans against the jamb, hips slouched, arm raised to glug from a plastic bottle of water. Above the collar of his damp T-shirt, his neck is slick with sweat, and his flushed skin looks plucked. He drinks, then pulls the bottle from his mouth, wipes his lips. "What are you doing?"

I'm pulling T-shirts from the drawer. An open duffel rests on the bed. "I'm going to stay with Bridget for a night or two."

"Is she okay?"

"Yeah, fine. We just talked this morning and decided it. We're going to rent movies, order in pizza, stay up late and highlight our hair. You know. Girl stuff."

He walks into the room, lifting his shirt to cool his skin. "I guess we can live without each other for another night or two."

"Two days a week, I think we can manage." A handful of cotton underwear fits in the duffel next to the shirts, and I push in two rolls of socks.

"Are you planning on making this a regular thing?" He puts the bottle down on the dresser and pulls his socks from his feet, tossing them toward the hamper.

"Every week for a month. See, this great opportunity opened up for me at the library, but I need to do training at the Civic Center. Excuse me," I say, and open the top drawer.

He moves back. "What great opportunity?"

I fish for a belt, pull it out and coil it around my finger, tuck it next to the socks. "There's a kids' workshop in San Rafael, and I might be able to start one here, combined with a nature program, but I need to train first. Adele's letting me do it, but I need to be in San Rafael every week."

"That *is* great," he says. "But what about the *Pilot*?"

"Murray was okay about it. I told him he could have my notes once you guys fact-checked them."

He picks up the bottle and tilts it against his mouth, but the water dams against his closed lips. He pulls the bottle away. "You could commute. San Rafael's not that far."

I shake my head.

His pale feet, swirled with white blond hair on the toes, stand on the floor at the end of the bed. I look up at the crease in his forehead. "When was the last time I got away?"

"We went to Monterey last month."

"We went. For a conference. For you."

"Yeah, but you came with. You had a good time."

"Did I?"

"What the hell is going on, Kit?" He does a small spin, away from me, and slams the bottle of water on the top of the dresser. His shirt, BIOLOGISTS DO IT WITH MORE LIFE, is faded gray from many washings and the thin fabric clings to the sweaty skin between his shoulder blades. He turns around again to look at me. "Why haven't you told me anything about this until now?" He points at the duffel, and his face crumples.

"We haven't had much time lately."

"Don't blame the lab." He nods, short jerky juts of his chin, and then shakes his head slowly. "You've known from the beginning it would be a full-time deal."

"This isn't about the lab."

"You're right." His hand is in his hair, pushing it back from his damp forehead. "I know I haven't been around. Frankly, it's been a lot easier at the lab. Every time I've tried to talk to you, you shut me out."

"So now it's my fault."

"Jesus, Kit. You're always picking a fight."

My voice is soft, almost a plea. "We moved here for you, Jeff."

"You wanted to move here as much as I did. Let's get that straight."

Jeans fit in last, stuffed at the top, and I zip the duffel closed. Its tight sausage shape makes me want to cry. "It's your work, Jeff. We came here for your work."

"But you raved on and on about Bodega Bay, about the wildflowers in spring, about the bay at low tide. Look at me." He grabs my arm. "You wanted this."

His hair sticks up, crazy, as if his fingers were still in it.

"Yeah, you're right. I did."

"Don't you want it anymore?" His hand is still on my arm, hard, but his eyes are narrowed into slits, the way he looked at me the first time we made love. "Don't you?"

"I do want it, Jeff. But I want other things, too." I sit on the bed and stare at his feet. It was easier to talk when I had something to do. "I never knew it could be harder to get something back than to lose it in the first place."

"Yeah, I know," he says. "I want things, too." His voice is quiet now, and when I look up at his face, the only red spots left are circles high on both cheeks. "I want us to be happy. I love you."

I nod, let my face go. Jeff sits down, and the duffel rolls into my hip from his weight next to me. We hold each other as the room darkens, and when we begin to kiss, I feel my body responding. Maybe we can cover up with this, with skin against skin. But what happens feels more like peeling back than covering up, and I am suddenly desperate for him, and when we are done, when we have come together, I still have myself. And then I tell him: "I love you."

Jock, in the doorway, cocks his head, lifts an ear, whines. "Don't worry, boy," I cry. "We're not going anywhere."

•

I walk down the hall. Past the posters, past the vending machines with their bright colors glowing on the plastic pressure panels—the blue and red swirl of the Pepsi logo, the orange and yellow of Minute Maid juices. The cement walls are cold as my knuckles brush against them. I imagine this place in hundreds of years, the labs abandoned, the scientists moved on, the humming and whirring of the internal furnace quieted. The walls will still be here, but they will no longer contain the stuff of science, of beakers, of Petri dishes, of tanks. Grasses will push up through cracks in the floor, roots down through holes in the ceiling; the rush and retreat of water will make geometric tidepools of the basement labs, their walls and counters obstacles no more than the rocks and bluffs of the shoreline.

Jeff's office is empty. The afternoon sun, so bright and white this time of day, is held back by a shiny green shade that has been pulled halfway down the huge window. The stools are pulled out from the counter, pencils left to roll and rest against coffee-stained mugs and thick piles of printout, monitors flashing screen savers. I weave through the abandoned stools and past a tank of marine grasses and reach into my pocket for the papers I have brought. I place them— notes, two sketchy attempts at an article, Murray's phone number—on top of a chart filled with tiny numbers in Jeff's precise hand. I ruffle the pages, and look up at a poster of native grasses hanging on the wall. Their likenesses have been painstakingly rendered in pen and ink, a wash of light color. Some are silvery, others more gold.

My father stopped me on a trail once to show me the bright red leaves, always three, of poison oak; another time the surprise of a buckeye pod, smooth and warm brown, as if lit from within, that fell from its split casing as soft as a spaniel's ears. And after I looked at what he was showing me, I would look at his head next to mine and at the crinkles at the corners of his eyes as he turned toward me and smiled. His eyes were blue, a blue that went gray on sunny days.

Outside the window, the hulking cement water-intake valve looks like a bunker I once played in at Fort Cronkhite, and I can hear my childhood voice following his lead as we stood in the darkness, our shouts of delight echoing off the walls. I move closer and look at the sun shining unabashedly on the broad, flat sea.

Tell Me Something
I Don't Know

Rhoda calls every Sunday morning, just as I walk in from the corner bakery with a banana-blueberry muffin in a white bag, fat newspapers sliding against my hip. "Your brother," she begins, complete with heaving sigh. He's been pulled over for a broken brake light and the police found outstanding traffic violations, two crack vials smashed under the front seat. He bargained with a judge for a ninety-day drug program and dropped out after four weeks. He lost his job at a bicycle repair shop and got another, at a bagel store, but couldn't keep the hours. My father hired him to stock the hardware storeroom ("Ned was so neat as a child," Rhoda says, as if in justification), and came up short eighty-four dollars. Etc.

Now it's the house again, three times in two weeks. Rhoda describes for me the motion-detecting beams, the dowels in the window frames, the safe in front of which my dad kneels every night. Ned still gets in. "Your brother," she says, "must have the tread of an angel. I'm such a light sleeper." As if his only crime is not waking her up.

I hold the phone out as far as I can, listen to the rise and fall of her voice. The sun outside my window is all white glare, heat covering the city like a tarp.

MY BROTHER. WE USED TO BE LIKE *THAT*—THIRD FINGER crossed over index, in the soft place between knuckles, the sign girls use to seal promises, break them, too. Ned and I used to sleep in each other's beds, pick each other's scabs, and poke at the black pores in each other's ears, like chimps. We'd wake each other Christmas morning so neither would be first to the tree. Our mother, Lucy, never had time to wrap, just left the toys and puzzles and games in their packages, his by the chair, mine against the wall.

Lucy died ten years ago. Dad married Rhoda two years after that, the summer I went away to college. Four years later, on my graduation day, I looked over a sea of caps to find Ned—Ned whose eyelids I used to lift while he slept to look at the gleaming whites of his eyes, Ned whose hot stale breath on my cheek would wake me up to listen to his latest nightmare, Ned who led me by the hand the night of his second-grade open house to his Petri dish on the window sill, its masking tape label folded over where the sticky side got tangled in his eager fingers. I found him, sitting between Rhoda in bright red and Dad with his camera, showing me a face I couldn't read, punishment for having left him.

I'VE SEEN HIM BREAK IN. I KNOW HE'S GOOD. LAST CHRISTMAS, two months before the deal with the judge, I was running errands one afternoon in Rhoda's car. She and Dad were at the store, busy ringing up tinsel and hooks and rolls of wrapping paper. I'd shut the trunk and was reaching to push the button to the electric garage door when a flash of movement caught my eye. Ned, throwing a bag through the gap of sunshine onto the pavement outside, dropping and rolling his body under the door just before it clunked shut.

I knew the bag. I made it myself for Lucy on Mother's Day in fifth grade, wove the scratchy straw fibers and sewed on the bright pink and yellow flowers made from bunched tissue paper. Ned had jammed it so full (batteries, I found out later, and books and videos he sold on the street, things my father said weren't worth the fuss of doing anything about) that the straw looked lumpy, strained, as abused as I felt to see him treat it like that.

I kept what I'd seen to myself until after Christmas, trying to protect all of us, I suppose, and our notion of a happy, normal family, opening gifts. Ned got some Al Green and Bonnie Raitt CDs for me, a backgammon set for our father, handpainted mugs for Rhoda. I keep meaning to throw those CDs away, but I can't, as if doing so would betray Bonnie's pretty smile, Al's direct gaze, some vague notion of forgiveness and hope.

The bushes on either side of the garage door don't lose their leaves in winter and they're big enough to hide behind, so that whenever I look at them I see him there, crouched legs tense with readiness to run for the closing door as soon as the car reaches the corner. I thought telling might make them bland, benign bushes again, but Dad just pinched the bridge of his nose.

What kind of parent, Rhoda wants to know, turns in his own child?

Sometimes I don't answer. I listen to the phone ring seven, eight, nine times. She always tries again later.

Rhoda will ask, "So tell me what's happening with you. What's new and exciting? What fun things have you been up to?"

She's not being ironic. I should be out enjoying the city, having a good time, loving life, loving men, making friends. There's no room for anything to go wrong with me.

All I can say is Nothing. Not much. I don't have words for the rest. I've tried—I'm upset about Ned, worried about her and Dad—but her voice snaps like a cord. "Tell me about it."

SOMETIMES SHE PUTS MY DAD ON THE PHONE. "I'M OKAY, Daddy," I say. "How are you?" He's fine, working long hours, busy now at the store, last-minute gutter-cleaner-outers, a rush on swamp coolers. We talk about the heat, the weather predictions. We talk about anything but.

"You and your father," Rhoda says, "don't like to talk." But that's not it. We've never needed to. I knew my mother had died when my father came home, put the car keys in the dish by the front door like every other evening of my life, and sat down next to me on the couch, crossed his hands between his knees, bowed his head. It wasn't until I went to get him a glass of water that he began to sob.

My father and I would stand for hours side by side sanding the doll-house furniture he made for me out of scraps of wood, untangling lights and stringing them around the eaves, sorting nails and drill bits and nuts and bolts. *Your daddy's girl,* my mother used to say. *I've got Ned. Watch him now,* were her last words to me.

Once, he fell from a tree in the neighborhood park, and I ran, sneakers pounding, screaming for no one to touch him. Another time, a current swirling with grasses caught him innertubing, and I pulled him to me from the riverbank with a long stick. And, third, when his sled ran so fast into a log that his body flew off into a hole crusted brown with old ice, I dug him out with mittened hands.

RHODA HAS A THEORY. "NED'S NEVER RECOVERED FROM YOUR mother's death. And your father"—here her voice will lower— "your father can't deal with it because he hasn't dealt with Lucy's death, either."

I've lost fifteen pounds, wake every morning to dry heaves. I've been sleeping late, standing on street corners past three light changes, losing deadlines at work. I've been avoiding friends, turning down invitations. I haven't had a date in six months.

Here's my theory: There's no more of me to give away.

ONE YEAR THERE WAS A TENT IN THE MIDDLE OF THE PACKAGES under the tree, a tent we had to wait until summer to set up so that when June finally came and Dad staked it in the backyard grass, it was Christmas morning all over again. We slept in it three nights in a row, dragging out flashlights and books and boxes of cereal. We scared each other with stories of monsters and men who lived in the lilacs. We poked each other's bare stomachs and shrieked. I had to run in to pee, and on my way back out, running down the stairs, I stopped. There's a window in that stairwell, right over the backyard, right over the tent. Ned sat upright, moving a flashlight over a picture book, lighting up the tent with a white glow against which his small shadow moved. I stood and stared as if he were already far away.

RHODA'S THEORY, OF COURSE, IS FLAWED. IT WANTS TO LINK cause and effect too neatly, as if hurt and love and disappointment, intention and loss and effort, add up like figures in a column. She never comes right out and asks, but I know she wants an explanation. "You're such a good girl. Your father's such a fair man. Your mother, everything I've heard, sounds like a wonderful person. You all gave Ned nothing but love."

I came home one day, three years before my mother got sick, and found my doll house furniture snapped like kindling. In fifth grade I kept a blue diary with gold lettering and a small brass lock that, when forced, sprung open the pages, stuck the key so it wouldn't come out again. I saved my allowance in a plastic bank with graduated grooves for pennies, dimes, nickels, and quarters, a bank that broken, left shards on my bed.

Lucy had a knack with after-school snacks. Apple wedges, slices of cheese, yogurt mixed with jam never felt like healthful imperatives as much as tasty accompaniment to the conspiratorial fun of school-day afternoons, the three of us as easily balanced as a three-legged stool until Dad came home and Lucy got up from the table to go to him. One day he held a brown paper sack, for me. I slid off the chair, leaving my mother and brother to finish an apple, my mother slicing it in her strong-veined, blunt-nailed grasp, Ned's sneakered feet dangling under the table.

Dad and I climbed the stairs, past the window where the sunlit glare caught the lift of his knees, the swish of my skirt, as colors in the glass. I followed him down the hall and into my bedroom. I was a good apprentice, eager yet sober. *Here,* he might have said, opening the brown sack, or *Hold these,* and poured the small screws into my hand that I knew to hold palm up. I held the Phillips head, he drilled the holes. And then, because his fingers were big and clumsy, I pinched each screw in position as he tightened the lock against the door frame. He stood back, and I reached up, swung the plate, pulled the knob. It held. We may have shook hands—two partners, the job complete—even smiled. I squirmed with satisfaction that night at the dinner table, as if Ned's being locked out of my room made up for knowing it was the only consequence he'd get, both too little and too much.

"WENDY," RHODA SAYS, AS SHE HAS BEFORE, "YOU MIGHT BE able to get through to Ned. He always listened to you." And then, because she needs the ballast, "Your father and I only thought."

I open my mouth, shut it, remember how Lucy would draw our bath at night, her hands cupping falling water, adjusting knobs, skimming the water's surface not yet hazed with soap or bobbing with hard-edged toy boats, plastic cups. "All yours," she'd say, patting the tub's edge, and stand up, leave us. We'd sit front to back, taking turns manning the spigots, filling the plastic cups. The victim had to choose a cup without knowing which tap had filled it. Ned's back was pale and fragile as he hunched in anticipation of scalding hot or icy cold. We played at hurt then, only a game, as if it could prepare us for when it would be the real thing.

He can call me. If he has something to say.

Rhoda repeats my name, sighs, clicks off.

I hold the phone. The glare presses tightly against the window. The walls are blank, the floor sticky against my bare feet. I imagine Rhoda, padding on pile carpet, bringing my father another iced tea. I see her pat his shoulder, him reach up and touch her hand. The dial tone sets in, then urgent beeps. Soon, they will go silent, and I will stand here, alone with the walls and the floor and the window, the glare that promises more of the same tomorrow. I hold the phone, waiting.

like This

I HAVE JUST LIFTED THE SANDWICH FOR MY FIRST BITE OF FOOD in twenty-four hours when I see my sister. My gut clenches. The back of my mouth tingles, like tin foil against fillings. It's my sister. There, across the street, almost halfway down the block, walking east, a purse strap slashed across her back, that loping awkward gait in flat shoes that scuff the sidewalk with each step. Shoes, I know from that day I hid in her closet after hearing the garage door open when I'd been getting high in the bathroom, that wear along the outside of the heels as if shaved. I crouched among them in the dark that day, fingers fumbling against wafer-thin soles, against tangled straps and buckles, against insoles curled stiff from dried sweat, and batted away the dresses and skirts that clung to my shoulders and cheeks.

The last time I saw my sister, Christmas, I was clean. Almost three months clean, and I'd make it another two and a half weeks before my birthday when I got back together with Carla, her mouth and hair over me so quickly, so lightly,

I didn't have time to think beyond how good she felt and before I knew it we're headed to Hayes Valley, a voice like a drum beat *Just this once*, and then the rush picks up, excitement and adrenaline but relief too that now I can stop watching for it out of the corner of my eye, now I'm facing it head on. And when Dee recognizes the van, grins and walks over, her hand already in her pocket, the voice beats on, *You're strong enough now, just this once, you can walk away later*, and I can almost believe it, almost believe that I have a choice, and then Dee calls out, "Hey, Wade—been a while, good to see you." I've always liked Dee. We make each other laugh. I tell myself, *She's your friend, relax*, my hand on Carla's leg, grinning back at Dee, lifting my hips to reach for a twenty, Dee's fist a blossom in her pocket, a blossom around the vial she pulls out as soon as she grasps the cash, and then Dee's gone, the blossom only brown fingers that dropped a skin-warmed plastic vial in my palm, a vial I don't even look at but pass to Carla as I press the gas pedal and take my hand off Carla's leg and the voice begins again, quieter now but more insidious, so I drive fast and hard as if I'm just in a hurry, running street names through my brain with each green light, each corner, but I know what it's saying, I know with every bone in my body the despair lining its words, *You're not strong, that's the white rock talking, you're the weakest son of a bitch that ever crawled on his belly, you're walking only in your dreams. In your dreams.* At the quiet end of the park I pull the van along the curb so we can smoke, sleep.

Christmas. Six or seven months ago. I know it's summer now because the surf at Ocean Beach no longer gets tangled and furious the way it does when storms back up in the Pacific. The last time we parked out there was before I sold my board, now even the parking lot at China Beach mocks me with its memory of winter's north swell, Fort Point just around the Gate, seeing the ocean when you can't surf hurts like the itch of an amputated limb. I know it's summer because the fog blows in so fast over my head and through the trees along Park Presidio, so thick I can barely see across the tops of the cars to the other side of the street. But I don't know if it's June or July. I don't even know what day it is. They all pass in a kind of sameness. Every night before I fall asleep I think, *Tomorrow I'll get myself across town to Dry Dock*, and stare at Carla's head on the cushion I ripped from the front seat and then wrapped in a T-shirt to make her a pillow, *tomorrow I'll go out to get food and won't come back*, and squeeze my eyes shut as soon as I find myself noticing how small and delicate her head is, as sleek as a seal's with its fine black hair that I can't help but reach out and touch. Every morning I wake to daylight seeping through the roof of the van like a 30-watt bulb through a shade, hunger so loud in my body it's all I hear, and by the time I have scrounged money for a muffin, or stolen bread and fruit from the shelf of a store, all resolution is gone in the rumble of my stomach, the self-loathing that begins at the first bite and ends only at night, back in the van again, when tomorrow can be anything because I'm not in it yet.

Christmas, my mother had six oysters for each of us, on ice all day in the refrigerator. I gulped mine down, briny, plump, while my sister watched me. Our father lifted his glass, I sipped soda while they all sipped wine, closed my eyes to say the serenity prayer and opened them to find she was still watching me, the gray-blue irises of her eyes gone flat in a way that would infuriate me when she stared right through me when I told her a joke or called her by one of our old child-hood nicknames. Used to be that was all it took to make her laugh, sometimes just a raised eyebrow, a mimicked adult stance, and we'd be off together in a language no one else spoke. I don't know when she got wary on me, but she did, and one Thanksgiving weekend when she was home from col-lege, I taunted her by counting how many times she said "Oh well" or "Whatever," as if her will had shrunk so much her only response could be equivocation. I looked away then in disgust at how easily she had given up, on herself I thought. But at Christmas I was sober, knew better. Across the laden table I met and held her stare, remembering not only the laughter but the comfort she'd had in her as a young girl, a comfort offered like a lap to crawl into even as I couldn't stay.

Carla will never come with me into recovery. She says it's weak, nothing but men sitting around all day watching TV, so passive they don't even hit the mute button when the commercials come on. She says all I need is a job so we can get out of this shitty van, live like people again. I tell her that in most of the programs there are donated black and whites that don't even have remote controls, and she says *That's not the point Wade*, her voice getting tight and screechy. Where's my loyalty? How can I leave her again? What would she do all alone? One night I did leave: jumped up, hopped out of the back of the van, slammed the door, and ran down Funston toward California. I'd gone three blocks when she caught up, driving up on the curb and screaming out the window so I had to get back in. She had all four tires back in the street for another block, and then pulled over outside a Union 76, lowered her head, unzipped my jeans with her teeth, half promise half threat. She's already got enough to hold over me, but I can always give her more.

There's traffic on Park Presidio day and night, and in the afternoon, after we've eaten, I move the van to a new spot on the quiet side of the trees and walk away, leaving Carla sleeping in the back, hugging the T-shirt pillow, her skin pale from being outside only at night, until I can't see the van anymore. I sit against a eucalyptus tree and brush tattered strips of fallen bark, smell the fog before I see it. My sister and I traveled this way as kids, going to the airport or, more frequently, to our grandfather's house. We would climb into the way-back on the way home, the empty back seat between us and our parents as if we were in a separate vehicle. In warm breath, she'd spin stories about how the street lights were runway signals to a secret land, a place we were going where we'd never been, like Oz, she'd say. "Doesn't it look that way?" she'd whisper, and then, "Shh...." And then we'd pull onto the bridge where the fog smudged the lights into golden blurs, and she was right, it did look that way, but what I noticed, above the lights, were the thick twisted cables that reached up into the fog. I had to know what was up there. I heard the rushing sound of other cars around ours, felt the car sway as our father changed lanes or braked, and knew that the back seat could not contain me—any more than my sister's imagination could. I had to burst ahead of the rest of the traffic, to soar and race, to break the confines of speed limit and traffic signals. Why? my parents would ask me years later as they waited with me on the cracked plastic chairs of juvenile hall. What, a judge once asked, would make a kid like you break the law? At sixteen I climbed the north tower, grabbing the cables and running until I was out of headlight reach. No fog that night so the lights were blurred only by tears from the wind, nothing above me at last but the stars.

"Let's pretend," she'd sometimes say, "let's pretend we've been kidnapped," and we'd sit up and mouth Help out the back window at the car behind us, falling against each other in laughter until our father called out to quit it. Then we'd quietly press our mouths to the glass and stick out our tongues, wanting not so much a response from the other drivers—who either smiled and waved or looked away, mouths set in grim lines—as to prolong our feeling of power over them, of invulnerability as we distracted them. By my junior year in high school I was a regular at juvenile hall, and the one time my sister drove me up there we said nothing the whole way, except for when we pulled alongside a pick-up, its cab big enough for a back seat. Three small faces grimaced and eyeballed out the rear window, three mouths stretched like anemones on glass at the aquarium. "Pass them," I told her, but she said, "No, I don't want to, I'm already going sixty." "Live a little," I told her. "Go sixty-five." She shook her head and waited a mile or two, tugging me on a short leash because then she did pass, and I turned my face to the window, pulled back my lips, touched my tongue to the tip of my nose, and waggled my eyebrows. Two kids pulled back in amazement, but the older one gleamed with delight. "Future delinquent of America," I said, but she only stared ahead, and I ached to grab the wheel, jerk us free.

The fog's thickest late in the day, when the birds start wheeling over the tops of the cypresses in Golden Gate Park. Seven I was or maybe eight one summer day when we stood in line for hours, eating hot dogs and popcorn balls, my mother and sister and I. Inside the Van Gogh exhibit at last, my mother stopped at the one of ivy, swirls of green paints so thick on the canvas they stood up. My sister liked the sunflowers best, but I couldn't stop staring at the one next to it. Crows, blots of jagged black against a field of gold. Years later, flipping channels late at night, too amped to sleep, when Carla and I still had an apartment, color TV, and cable, I caught it on A&E, filling the screen. I learned then that it was the last painting Van Gogh did before killing himself, and it made perfect sense, how loud and mocking those circling crows would be until you could paint them, but how painting them might be worse because then they'd exist outside of you, too. Carla'll sleep for another hour, but I run back to the van to crawl next to her, burrow into her hair, touch the narrow tight ribcage under the drum of her skin. She'll hold me and murmur my name, not call me weak. And later, when she'll ask me to score more, we'll pass the park on our way downtown and they'll be just birds again.

"HEY PAL," I TOLD THE MAN'S BLANK, WIDE, ASIAN FACE, "don't wrap it. I'm going to eat right away." But he did, swaddling the sandwich tightly in butcher paper, even taping it. I slapped the money on the counter. Bastard didn't even meet my eyes. Everywhere I go they smell it on me, storekeepers and dealers and cops. I'd never rip this store off. I'd go farther away, someplace I've never eaten a sandwich, chatted up an old lady. I'm in the blistering sunshine, the door jangling behind me, its glass panel covered with a Newport ad of a laughing couple tugging a football like a bad joke, when I rip off a corner of paper and lift the roll. When I see her, the bread turns to cardboard on my tongue. My sister lives in L.A., has a job, a nice apartment, a life so different from mine it's as if we never lay side by side in the back of the car but I know we did, it's what makes my heart stop when I see her, stop and then start pounding. It's not her. It's her.

She walks like my sister, steady and upright but without straightening her legs at the back of each stride, as if she were wearing heels and a tight skirt. My sister would never wear heels and a tight skirt, not during the day, not on the street. I usually don't notice women dressed in loose skirts and baggy sweaters, their fineness all hidden away in folds and drapes. If I could see the curve of her jaw I'd know. At the corner, she stops, lifts her knee and rubs her calf as though she pulled a muscle, tore a tendon. Her hair hangs straight down. The narrow ribcage, the long waist. She's always moved as though her center of gravity were somewhere above her shoulders. She trips easily, can't ski, could never surf. But she's grown into her body, I see as I watch her cross the street, turning her head in one direction but not the other so I still can't see the slice of profile that would tell me for sure, moving with the fulcrum of her weight now between her hips, as though she carries a bowl balanced there, a bowl brimming with liquid that sways a little with each step but does not spill. I can't lose her now.

It hurts to squint into harsh white sunlight, hurts to chew the roast beef on French roll that I spent four of my last seven bucks on, hurts to feel my stomach pull the food down and cramp for more. Carla's going to wake up soon, hungry too, maybe remembering that I whispered into her tangled black hair before leaving, "Be right back," maybe not, starting to scrounge through my jacket pockets, my knapsack, the glove compartment, to see if I have money squirreled away that I haven't told her about, to see if I've kept anything from her that we could hock. But I keep scuttling crookedly along the storefronts of Sacramento Street, following this apparition, this stranger, this sister, as she walks confidently down the center of the sidewalk. Loss breaks over me, no longer with the crisp edge of an approaching cresting wave but with the rushing tumble of one that has crashed right on top of me, and I bend over, my stomach jolting in revolt as I hack up chewed roast beef and French roll and the tang of sweet mustard and bitter saliva. I spit, wipe my mouth with the back of my hand. I can't let her see me like this.

She crosses Baker and heads north, her swinging skirt flashing the pale back of a calf with each uphill step, each bent knee. She is slowing down, fumbling with her purse. I crouch behind a parked Civic. Her hair falls forward as she bends her face down toward her open purse, and then she pushes it back behind her ear, a move I have seen my sister make thousands of times, and suddenly looks up. Perhaps after three blocks she senses she is being followed. Perhaps she is as nervous as the man behind the deli counter at my presence, although it is late morning on a sunny day, although we are in one of the city's safest neighborhoods. Perhaps, as she lifts her keys from her purse and sweeps the street with her gaze, she notices my feet as an irregular shadow between the regular shapes of the Civic's back tires. Perhaps. But it doesn't matter, because in the instant before I jerk my head back behind the car I have seen what I need to know.

On those visits to our grandfather, Poppa always gave us each a new penny, then as we got older a crisp dollar bill, asking each time, "How much have you saved now?" My sister, having counted before we left the house, would reply with the exact amount she kept in a papier-mâché box she'd made in school. Sometimes I'd go into her room and lift the lid to marvel at the bills tucked neatly along the box's folded edge, coins covering the bumps of dried glue. I never stole from her, not so much because I knew how carefully she tracked her money but because I was in a kind of awe at her thrift, as if we were separate species and I was learning about her unique money saving habits on the Discovery Channel. One day she told Poppa, "Eight dollars and forty cents," and he patted her head—"That's a girl"—and turned expectantly to me. I had no idea, I'd spent some of it, lost some of it, and never remembered to count what I did have, but I said "Four dollars and twenty cents," thinking that since I was half her age at the time I would have accumulated half as much. He smiled, and I can remember the sour disappointment at being praised for something I hadn't done when the calculation I had done was much more remarkable, but I couldn't announce it without admitting the lie. His watery blue eyes held mine a fraction longer than usual, and I wondered suddenly if he was on to me. If his failings that my parents talked about on the drive home—forgetting my mother's name, abruptly interrupting my father once to ask "And who are you?"—were tricks he played on them, and if he could see through to deeper truths.

I wondered if he knew what I'd done, and if it was okay. But already it was my secret, something to keep me apart, and I said nothing.

I stumble, fall to the curb, almost drop the sandwich. There is a brief moment of clarity where the trip to Dry Dock is a bus ride I can catch a block away, where I do not hear the rushing outside the station wagon or the drum beat inside of me, where I can stay with my sister, a brief moment before what could have been tumbles against the bruised tissue of my brain and I wrap up what is left of the sandwich to take back to Carla, knowing I'll be ahead by three dollars if I don't have to buy her one of her own.

Careful

THEY HAD NOTHING IN COMMON. SHE TAUGHT AN EVENING poetry workshop at the local community college and worked as a translator from the French during the day. He was doing a postgrad in physics, spending hours with strings of numbers and symbols as strange to her as hieroglyphics. She could barely move in the morning until she had the first of three cups of coffee (a blend long ago perfected, ground from beans in the first harsh noise of her day); he could emerge from four hours' sleep with only a glass of juice or an apple, and nap on the sidelines of a basketball game. She wore a lot of black—turtlenecks, leggings, mini skirts with opaque tights, boots; he dressed in jeans and a T-shirt with a button-down unbuttoned over it, sneakers on his big feet. She talked a lot out of nervous habit, finishing many sentences with "you know?" or "don't you think?" He always answered, but measured his own questions with care and consideration, as if he might have a limited amount and didn't want to use them up too soon. When they spoke on the phone, his voice, deep and smooth with an even, soft laugh, carried the echo of their intimacy, his familiarity with the feel and scent of her skin, so that even when they were discussing the bridge traffic and if she should take an alternate route, she was reminded of what they did together in bed.

SHE TOLD ALL HER FRIENDS IT WAS A FLING, NOTHING MORE. She got an itchy feeling when she talked too much about him, as if she might be making something up. When her friend Ian ran into them together one night at a concert and referred to him the next day as the Puppy, she agreed that he did remind her of an eager, loping golden retriever. She had always preferred cats.

IN BED, HE WAS ALMOST NOISELESS. She knew from the acceleration of his breathing, the tightening of his runner's thighs, the increased rhythm of his thrusts, when he was going to come, but the only time he made a cry or moan was when she took him in her mouth. "You know why I like doing that?" she'd say, and he'd shake his head, perplexed that she needed to ask about everything, even this. For him it was enough that she used only her lips, that she always finished what she began. "I want to hear you. I want you to be noisy. It's all those years of dorm living, isn't it? Those walls thin as cardboard?"

He'd blushed then. She was this straightforward only in bed, where she said things no lover of his had ever said, where she wasn't squeamish about the mess of sex. "When you hold my hand," she told him the first night they slept together, "it makes me wet." She looked at him so hard sometimes when she was on top that he closed his eyes.

His favorite foods were things she could easily live without (spaghetti with bolognese sauce, salmon baked in butter and bread crumbs, clam chowder), while the foods she loved (sushi, dim sum, baba ghanoush) made him wrinkle his nose like a boy. There was a lot about him that was like a boy, she thought the first time she watched him jog onto the basketball court, a paper cup from Starbucks between her feet on the bleachers step, her hand raised in its leather glove when he looked her way and grinned. He didn't look over at her once the game started, and she loved watching how his body moved apart from hers, up and down the court, how he frowned with concentration, his hair falling into his eyes. When the whistle blew and he came to sit at her feet, his skin slick with perspiration under the bright lights of the gym, and leaned his elbows on her thighs, she pulled his head back by his damp hair and kissed him between the eyes.

SHE LIKED THE SECURITY OF WORDS, OF TURNING A PAGE AND finding more. She could tighten and refine, but she was still moving from word to word, a smooth exchange of commodity. Sometimes she would dream of a shape made from lines on a page—an hourglass, a staggered step ladder, a justified block of prose—and would awaken to think of the words with which she could fill it, as if pouring water into a vessel. His questions were becoming more personal—"How did your father die?" one night as they'd been eating ice cream on the couch and she'd been wondering whether or not to bring him to a gallery opening, and "Are you two still close?" another time after she'd parenthetically mentioned her favorite cousin's suicide attempt in a longer story about her uncle's career as a private eye. When silence fell between the two of them, she grew agitated, her mind a colony of uncertainty, questions and doubts multiplying exponentially like reproducing insects during every second in which nothing was said until the silence became alive with their buzz. His questions scared her.

SHE LOVED THE WAY HE'D ORDER TWO PLATES WHEN THEY
went out to breakfast together—French toast and an omelette
with hash browns. The customers at the next table would raise
their eyebrows and nudge one another when the waitress
brought over the order, and she'd flush with pleasure. He was
like an oven, a furnace, that after a night with her needed refu-
eling. When she crawled into bed and pressed up against him,
he yowled at her cold feet and took them between his hands
to warm them, rubbing their smooth skin, their scalloped
arches, as her black hair fell against his arm, as her mouth
moved across the back of his neck.

TRANSLATION HAPPENS AT THREE LEVELS, SHE REMINDED
herself when beginning a new job. First, the literal, word for
word substitution (*J'ai froid* = I have cold), next the level of
fluency, where meaning transcended mere literality (I am
cold), and then the intuitive, emotional level, where she
entered the logic of the language, its sensibility (what it means
for cold to be something you have instead of something you
are). For the first level, she needed only a dictionary; anyone
could do it, but as customers of Chinese restaurants know,
accuracy often suffered. For the second level, she had to know
the nuances of usage and grammar, the language's rules and
exceptions. As for the third—well, that was where translation
lifted above the level of mere substitution of one word for
another and entered the realm of culture, humanity. That was
the level on which she was drawn to him, the level where she'd
felt certain his numbers and symbols must take him. While
she struggled to fill the shapes of poems, he sat at the computer, inputting figures that yielded parabolas and waves and
the gorgeous, Spirograph-like flowers of polar axes. She'd seen
his notes for a lecture on mechanics, scrawled equations that
lessened the gulf between a falling sphere and a solid plane the

way words could bridge the gap between people and fill spaces limitless with possibility.

WHEN THEY'D BEEN TOGETHER ALMOST THREE MONTHS, HE called out her name one night in bed. She'd collapsed on his chest, splayed over him, listening to the watery beat of his heart, and was suddenly aware of her own weight, her perspiration and dampness, the garlic and clams she'd eaten five hours earlier. She couldn't look at him, didn't lift her head. He squeezed her upper arms and ran his hands along her waist, down her hips, stroked the backs of her knees, and told her she'd stiffened. "Look at me," he said, and she did, but then kissed him so she could close her eyes, so she didn't have to see how he watched her. He said her name again, and eased out from underneath her to turn on his side, fold her body into his, whisper into the tangle of her dark hair. Before this, she would've murmured a "Hm?" or "What's that?", would've said something to hedge the silence, the rush of confusion and awkwardness she felt, but now she waited for him to fall asleep, and then slid out of bed to sleep on the couch. In the morning when she opened her eyes to see him naked next to her, she said she'd been restless, had a bad dream, moved so not to disturb him. He picked up her hand then, rubbed it in his, studied it as if he'd never before noticed that she, too, had five fingers.

THEY HAD THEIR FIRST ARGUMENT WHEN SHE TOOK A RUSH job for the end of March, for the week he had vacation. "I just assumed you'd be out of town," she told him without meeting his eyes. "Or running around, with friends."

He peered at her, cocked his head. "We talked about it. We talked about going hiking. Remember?"

"It was completely abstract. It slipped my mind, and when they called about this job, I didn't have anything written on the calendar so I forgot," she lied. The truth was, she'd had a flash so vivid she could see the colors on the magazine page: an article she'd seen in *Cosmopolitan* months—years?—earlier. *Never call him just to say hi.* It was number three on a list, "Ten Steps to Make Him Yours." "I need the money, you know. I don't have a regular stipend like some people."

"Okay," he said cheerfully. "I see what you're doing."

"What?"

"I'm not going to take your bait. I don't want to argue."

"Argue? Who said anything about arguing? I don't want to either." They were standing in her kitchen, and she leaned forward to tug on his belt loop, raise her eyebrows. Somewhere on the list was *Be hot in bed, and cool out of it.* He pulled back so her fingers slipped free, and looked down, nodding. In bed, on the court, his frown was softened by reddened cheeks, a slackened mouth—but this look was sharper, more discerning, the way she imagined he looked when figuring out a complex problem, the answer latent in the numbers all along.

"I thought of you today," she said hurriedly. "There was a billboard for some bank, and it had those angular Ss, what are they, sigmas? In an equation?"

"Summations."

"I guess so. Yes, and those numbers between lines, like parentheses but straight? What are those?"

"Absolute value."

"Yes."

The frown didn't decrease, and as she tried to explain— "all those mathematical symbols, you know, they made me think of you"—it only got worse. After all, he'd never told her he'd thought of her because he saw a sentence.

HE LIKED WHAT HER FRIEND STEPHANIE REFERRED TO AS testosterone films, the kind of loud, nonstop action movies that gave her a headache. She searched the listings every week for revivals of *Chien Andalou, Zero de Conduite, Les Enfants de Paradis,* movies to which he accompanied her until, distracted by the shifting and crossing of his long legs in the bouncy seats of the Rialto and the Vogue, she stopped bringing him along.

She found and attended more gallery openings, readings, poetry slams, standing around small, crowded, smoky rooms, striking a balance between allure and boredom. She signed up at Open Mike Nights, reading in a clear, strong voice to a spot in the audience she imagined as his thatch of thick blond hair and telling herself the only reason she hadn't invited him was because she knew how uncomfortable he'd be in the rickety folding chairs. She attended another basketball game, but bowed out of the party afterward, claiming a headache. When he loped over to her after scoring the winning basket and accepting the hugs of his teammates, she lifted her face and a bead of sweat fell from his nose onto her cheek, where he rubbed it into her skin.

"LET'S GO CAMPING," HE SUGGESTED ONE DAY ON THE PHONE, and when she fluttered the pages of a preface to a new anthology of contemporary French poetry and said "I don't know the first thing about camping," he responded, "That's okay. I do."

"I don't even have a sleeping bag, or a backpack," she said, too, but he wouldn't take the hint, and when she joked that all she could contribute was a can of chili her old roommate had left behind, he said, "Great. I'll pick you up at three." They were in the National Seashore parking lot by five, nervous at their first trip together and hyper after huge bear claws at the bakery in town. *Make his interests yours* would have been toward the top of the *Cosmopolitan* list.

During the three-mile hike through the woods to the coast, she let her hand hang loose at her side so he might pick it up, swing it, smile at her. They passed quite a few trees, at any of which he could have stopped her, leaned her against the rough bark, kissed her. By the time they reached camp she had to pee, and when she emerged from between the dunes, he'd already set up the tent. Inside it, a lantern was lit, sending his shadow looming against the tent's fabric walls. She pulled the flap aside and leaned in to tell him he was missing the sunset. The sleeping bags had been shaken out and placed side by side, and between them sat the lantern, a guidebook on coastal wildflowers, and two glossy green apples.

"Separate beds?"

He looked at her as he passed through the tent opening as if she were suggesting something rash, something that violated safe camping codes.

"I think they zip together," she said as she plowed behind him through the heavy sand to the beach.

"I thought it might be a good idea," he answered, "if we didn't sleep together for once." He'd turned his head toward her as he spoke, but there was enough of a wind for her eyes to water and she looked away, pretending she hadn't heard. Of course. Why hadn't she seen it sooner? Not a dinner for two with candlelight and her prettiest dress, no flowers, no good wine sipped in front of a fireplace, no soft rug where he'd cover her belly with kisses and she'd arch up to him, again and again. *If he loves you, he won't be able to keep his hands off you.*

The setting sun smeared pink and yellow on the ocean horizon. She hated following him, hated watching him jump off a dune onto the firmer sand below, hated the fact her feet had to move into the indentations his had made. She had to put her hand down to steady herself. They walked to the edge of the water, and she looked out and wondered how far she could swim before cramp and cold caught up. Five fishing boats moved slowly northward, and she imagined how the two of them might look from decks glistening and slippery with nets of fish. Tiny dots on the edge of the continent.

"It's beautiful," he said, and raised his arms, stretched. "I'm so glad we're here." He draped his arm around her shoulder. It felt friendly, affectionate. "You cold?"

"A little."

"Here." He bent his head forward to pull off his sweater.

"No," she said, stopping him with her hand and then pulling it away, dusting off the sand that clung to her palm. "I'll go get something."

He nodded. "I'll be right along to get the fire started."

She scooted back over the dunes, and when she'd dipped down below them and out of the wind, she looked back but both he and the sea were no longer visible. The sky glowed violet.

Socks, she remembered as she knelt and dug through the knapsack for another sweater. She'd had a vision of socks when he'd first said the word camping. She'd seen them thick and woolly against her narrow feet, baggy around her small-boned ankles, as she propped her feet in his lap as they sat around the fire, and curled them against his in a toasty pocket of sleeping bag. The wool socks made a safe structure in which to tell herself a story, like the lines of poetry she dreamed of, but this image wasn't filling out the way it was supposed to. The gap between the real and the imagined was everywhere, unavoidable.

Walking back toward him as he expertly started the fire and leaned back on his heels as if he'd been born that way to reach for a skillet, the can of chili, a baton of foil-wrapped French bread, she was suddenly terrified. He was a man with no interest in socks or candlelight or kissing her against a tree, a man with whom she was supposed to share a tent. He seemed utterly self-sufficient, completely without expectations. Worst of all, wool socks were such a lousy cliché.

AFTER DINNER THEY SAT SIDE BY SIDE ON THE BEACH, NOT even holding hands. She knew without looking that he'd reclined, lying down to watch the sky, as calm and relaxed as if her silence meant only that she didn't have to talk. She'd said little during dinner other than how good the food tasted cooked over an open fire, how bright the stars were away from the city—small talk that seemed brave to her now, valiant. She saw another picture, no socks in this one—just her body lying next to his, the way it would have before tonight, her head resting in the hollow between his chest and shoulder. She drew her knees tightly to her chest and propped her chin on her hands, shivered. When he spoke, his voice was almost a drawl, and she expected an astronomical observation, a story of the constellations, the ultimate mathematical anecdote. "Do you realize this is the longest time we've spent together without having sex?"

The sand lost all warmth as soon as the sun went down and now it shifted, cold, under her heels. As a child, she had been amazed to dig and dig at the beach and still find plenty of sand. It grew harder and wetter as you neared the water, but as you scraped your fingers through it, its fine texture and crumbly insubstantiality seemed to belie the solidity that held up not only the waves but the weight of the land.

"Think about it," he continued. "I picked you up at three, it's close to nine now. That's six hours. Usually, we'd be in bed."

She was glad for the space around them, the dark, the crashing waves. "You could have saved us a lot of trouble, you know."

"How's that."

"Backpacks and a drive up the coast and schlepping camping gear and putting up a tent seems like an awfully complicated way to tell me you don't want me anymore." She felt suddenly lighter, freer, as if she'd been holding her breath waiting for cold water and now that she was in it, she could swim away. When he spoke again, she was startled. She'd almost forgotten he was there.

"You're right. I did go to a lot of trouble."

The wind had died down, but she could feel the cool night air moving between them. His hand rested on the sand next to her foot, but their closeness was only of fabric, of the wool fibers of their sweaters reaching out in the dark. They'd sleep in the tent, backs curled away from each other, and awaken to sit silently over camp coffee, hike back, drive to the city. Her bones ached.

He lifted a fist of sand and then released it, small grains sprinkling her bare foot. "I guess it would have been easier to take you out for coffee and say what I've wanted to say."

She imagined holding out her hand, saying Stop, walking off, but instead she kept quiet and still, kept from making even the smallest move that might have disturbed the fine layer of sand dusting the top of her foot.

"I'm enormously attracted to you. Hugely. I love going to bed with you. I think you know that."

He'd lowered his voice, and she shut her eyes, suddenly shy not at the memory of his pleasure and her lack of inhibition but at the fact he was right next to her, as if this moment exposed her more than sex itself. "But lately I've been feeling like it's all we do. Like it's all you want to do. I've been wondering what might happen if we got to know each other out of bed." He sat up now, and spoke surprisingly close to her ear. "You see, a tent and sleeping bags were all part of my plan. You can't get out of bed here and go sleep on the couch." She heard the smile in his voice, and also the hurt.

"No, but I could grab the lantern and your keys, walk back to the parking lot, sleep in the car."

"You could."

"I could."

Words bridged gaps, as numbers measured them, but they also obscured meaning, blurred an idea and its realization if used sloppily, if translated carelessly. A good poem, like an algebra solution, had clarity to it because it had been reduced, all extraneousness canceled out, so that through its form pure content shone.

She bent her head back and took a deep breath, and when their hands clasped, tiny grains of sand pressed against both their palms. Distances dropped away in the darkness, and out beyond the breakers, a white path of moonlight stretched to the horizon.